A

KINCAID, J.D.

JUDGEMENT AT RED ROCK

Judgement at Red Rock

J.D. KINCAID

A Black Horse Western

ROBERT HALE · LONDON

© J.D. Kincaid 1993
First published in Great Britain 1993

ISBN 0 7090 5028 3

Robert Hale Limited
Clerkenwell House
Clerkenwell Green
London EC1R 0HT

To Dick and Hazel

Photoset in North Wales by
Derek Doyle & Associates, Mold, Clwyd.
Printed in Great Britain by
St Edmundsbury Press Ltd, Bury St Edmunds, Suffolk.
Bound by WBC Bookbinders Ltd, Bridgend, Mid-Glamorgan.

ONE

Boots Sutherland had chosen a dangerous profession, and he knew it. But the rewards were good, supposing a man lived long enough to enjoy them. And, so far, he had done just that.

Small and gnome-like, he sat hunched in the saddle, squinting against the morning sun. It was early and the sun was at an awkward height. Sutherland pulled the brim of his grey Stetson forward to shade his eyes.

Ahead of him, the trail wound its way through a narrow, boulder-strewn gulch. He smiled grimly. One thousand dollars. That was the price on Norton Kane's head, the reward Boots Sutherland intended claiming when he brought Kane in. He had followed the outlaw across two states, had almost caught up with him in Denver and then, on a couple of occasions, nearly lost his trail altogether. This time, however, there would be no mistake. This time he would surely catch up with the unsuspecting desperado and gun him down.

As this happy thought flitted through Sutherland's mind, he heard a familiar sound. The click of a rifle being cocked. And, to his consternation, the sound came from directly behind him. He whirled round, his right hand reaching for the Remington in his holster. But he was too late. He found himself staring down the barrel of a Colt Hartford revolving rifle. The man he had been pursuing had evidently spotted him and had lain in wait for him.

The outlaw stepped out from behind a tumble of rocks, an evil leer splitting his thin features. Sutherland's hand hovered uncertainly above the butt of his Remington. Then, as it closed round the gun's handle, Norton Kane fired. The Colt Hartford barked once, twice, thrice.

The first shot smashed through Boots Sutherland's rib-cage and punctured a lung, the second blasted a huge hole in his belly, and the third struck him in the throat, severing his jugular. The force of the three shots was such that it knocked Sutherland clean out of the saddle, and he landed flat on his back in the dust. As he lay there, he coughed convulsively, blood spurting up like a fountain from the severed vein. Norton Kane stood over him and spat contemptuously.

'Goddam bounty hunter,' he snarled.

A fourth shot between the eyes snuffed out what little life was left in Boots Sutherland's bullet-riddled body. Then Norton Kane calmly and unhurriedly reloaded the rifle and rammed it back into his saddleboot. And, without so much as another glance at his blood splattered victim, the outlaw mounted his horse and continued on his way through the gulch.

It was high noon and a blazing sun beat down on Norton Kane as he slowly approached the small Kansas cattle town of Red Rock. He slouched forward in the saddle and wiped a perspiring brow. His thin features contorted and he narrowed his eyes and scanned the almost deserted Main Street. He touched the sorrel's flanks and urged the horse forward along the dusty thoroughfare. The town was like a thousand or more other prairie settlements. But it had one significant advantage over the last few he had passed through. It was situated over the state line in Kansas, and Kansas was one state in which Norton Kane was not a wanted man.

He was wanted in two states for armed robbery and in three more for both armed robbery and murder. And he was tired of running. He seemed to have been running for nigh on five years, ever since he came out of Claxton County Jail and joined forces with the Grout brothers and Travis Miller and Spence Delroy to rob the Cattlemen's Bank in Cheyenne. Other robberies had followed in other states, and he had ridden hard and long to out-distance the law. But what had he to show for it? Not a goddam thing. The money he had taken, and there had been plenty of it, had all gone. It had either been spent on whiskey and loose women or lost at poker, blackjack and roulette. The result was, Norton Kane was darned near broke.

He reined in the sorrel outside Flanagan's Saloon and swung stiffly out of the saddle. Then he hitched the horse to the rail in front of the saloon and clattered up the half-a-dozen wooden steps to the stoop. He paused on the stoop, peered over the top of the batwing doors and carefully surveyed the interior.

Just like Main Street, Flanagan's Saloon was almost deserted. Noon mid-week in Red Rock was a pretty quiet time and the saloon had few customers. Four elderly poker players sat at a table in one corner of the bar-room and the town drunk slumped across one end of the marbled bar-top. The only other person present was the proprietor himself, Frank Flanagan.

A big, heavily-built man in a grimy white apron, Flanagan stood behind the bar, busily polishing beer-glasses. He watched the bank robber push open the batwing doors and make his way across the sawdusted floor. He didn't like what he saw, for his instincts told him that the stranger was likely to prove to be trouble. Consequently, he edged a little closer to the scatter-gun which he kept propped up behind the bar-counter.

What he saw was a man of medium height, a slim man dressed all in black and toting a Colt Peacemaker. But there was more. Norton Kane's thin face had a real mean look to it, his eyes as cold and grey as the Alaskan sea in mid-winter. A narrow black moustache decorated Kane's upper lip and, when he smiled, sharp, tobacco-stained teeth filled his rat-trap of a mouth. He leant against the marbled bar-top and lit a cheroot.

'Gimme a beer,' he rasped.

Frank Flanagan frowned. But he knew better than to refuse to serve the stranger. Covered in trail-dust and with his clothes travel-stained and badly worn, Kane might look like some penniless saddle tramp. Yet he had about him a positive aura of menace. And so Flanagan pulled the beer and slid the glass across the counter towards him.

'Come far?' enquired the saloon-keeper, endeavouring to act the part of the genial host.

'Far enough,' replied Kane curtly.

The gunslinger drained the glass at one go and then belched loudly. He grinned and slid the glass back across the counter towards Flanagan.

'Same again,' he snapped, tossing a few cents onto the marbled bar-top.

Flanagan pulled a second beer and hastily gathered up the outlaw's money. Thereupon, much to his relief, the black-clad stranger stepped away from the bar and carefully carried his beer across the bar-room to a table by the window, overlooking Main Street. The man's presence made Flanagan feel distinctly uneasy. Therefore, he was quite content that Kane should choose to remove himself to the opposite side of the saloon.

Norton Kane, for his part, wanted peace to think. He was down to his last few dollars. What should he do? Hold up Flanagan for his bar-takings, or maybe rob the local bank? He smiled thinly. Robbing Flanagan would be child's play. But, to make it worthwhile, he would have to

wait a few days, for he figured that Flanagan's
takings wouldn't amount to a row of beans
mid-week. The only time they would be worth
stealing would be on Saturday nights, when the
cowboys rode into town from the nearby ranches.
That was if the day-to-day routine at Red Rock
was the same as in the many other cattle towns he
had visited, and Kane had no reason to suppose it
was any different.

On the other hand, to attempt to rob the bank
singlehanded would be goddam risky. The smart
thing to do would be to enlist some help. He
straight away thought of his old pardners. The
last he had heard, the Grout brothers were in
Wichita, while Travis Miller and Spence Delroy
had been living it up in Dodge City. He reflected
wryly that they had made a pretty good outfit
before they had split up. Unfortunately, though, it
would take time for the others to reach Red Rock,
even supposing they were still where he figured
them to be.

That was the problem. Kane needed to act now,
before his last few remaining dollars ran out. He
swore beneath his breath and took a gulp of his
beer. Then he chanced to glance out of the
window. On the opposite side of Main Street was
the town's general store and, standing framed in
the doorway, was a tall, broad-shouldered fellow,
smartly dressed in a dark-grey, city-style suit and
sporting a green brocade waistcoat and bootlace
tie. The man was bareheaded and Kane noted
that his thick black hair was liberally speckled

with grey. He had handsome, square-cut features and Kane took him for a man in his late thirties or early forties. He was puffing nonchalantly on a cigar and looked to be one of Red Rock's more prosperous citizens. Kane guessed that he was, in all probability, the proprietor of the general store. Kane stared at the sign above the door. It proclaimed the owner to be one Benjamin Beardsley Esq.

A puzzled frown creased Norton Kane's brow. The man looked vaguely familiar, yet he knew nobody with that name. Benjamin Beardsley? Ben Beardsley? A light suddenly dawned and Kane stared hard at the storekeeper. The man was a lot greyer and a little heavier than when he had last seen him. But, then, that was ten years ago. And, at that time, he had gone under the name of Bradley, Ben Bradley.

Norton Kane chuckled to himself. The two men had met briefly in Claxton County Jail. They had shared the same cell for the last three weeks of Bradley's seven-year sentence and for the first three weeks of his, Kane's five-year sentence. He wondered idly whether Bradley's fellow-citizens knew of the storekeeper's unsavoury past. He rather suspected that they did not. Otherwise, why should Bradley have changed his name to Beardsley?

Kane turned and glanced across the bar-room at the saloon-keeper. He raised his hand and beckoned him. Flanagan scowled, put down the glass he had been polishing and reluctantly rounded the bar-counter and made his way across to where Kane was sitting.

'You wantin' somethin'?' he growled.

Kane smiled.

'Yeah. A li'l information.'

"Bout what?'

"Bout that dude standin' in the doorway of the store opposite.'

'What's he to you?'

'Nuthin'. I'm jest curious. He looks kinda rich an' influential. Guess he must be an important feller in this here town?'

'Yo're right there, stranger.'

'I am?'

'Yup. Ben Beardsley, he's the mayor of Red Rock.'

'A reg'lar of the community, huh?'

Frank Flanagan regarded the gunslinger with marked disapproval. He didn't like the man's tone. There was a sarcastic edge to it, even although the words in themselves were no way derogatory.

'Ben's a much respected citizen of Red Rock,' stated Flanagan. 'He's upright an' honest, he attends church regularly an' 'deed four years ago he married the preacher's daughter. They have two fine children, a boy an' a girl, whom he jest adores. Yeah, a real good family man is Ben.'

'I s'pose he makes a good livin' from that there store?' said Kane.

'From that, an' from the feed 'n' grain store an' the livery stables. Ben's done well durin' the ten years he's been in Red Rock. The town's grown an' Ben's grown with it.' Flanagan eyed Kane closely and asked, 'That satisfy yore curiosity, stranger?'

'Sure does. Thank you, mister.'

'My pleasure,' replied Flanagan, although, from the look on his face, it was plain that talking to Kane gave him no pleasure at all.

Kane remained at the table, slowly drinking his beer and watching the mayor through the saloon window. He noted that Beardsley had a word or two with everyone who passed the store, not that many of Red Rock's citizens had ventured out in the heat of the midday sun. Morning and late afternoon were the best times for trade. Nevertheless, Beardsley remained in the doorway for another half-hour or more, before eventually retreating into the comparative coolness of his store. As he did so, Kane finished his beer and rose from the table.

Before he could reach the batwing doors, Flanagan hailed him.

'Jest passin' through, are yuh, stranger?' the saloon-keeper enquired hopefully.

Norton Kane shook his head.

'Nope,' he said. 'I figure on stayin' around for a while.'

'If yo're lookin' for a job....' began Flanagan.

'I ain't lookin' for no job,' replied Kane, and he abruptly turned his back on the saloon-keeper and stepped out through the batwing doors.

He crossed the street and clambered up onto the sidewalk outside Ben Beardsley's general store.

Inside the store, the gloom forced Kane to pause a moment till his eyes adjusted. It was pleasantly cool, however, and Kane stood and gazed round the well-stocked emporium. There were no customers, only Beardsley and his clerk, a thin, bespectacled youth with a mop of tow-coloured hair, carefully parted and plastered down with water. Kane grinned and, picking his way through the merchandise, approached the wooden counter behind which the two men stood talking.

'Yessir, can I help you?' asked the youth.

Kane ignored him and, instead, addressed Ben Beardsley.

'Howdy, Ben. It's been a long time,' he said.

'You have me at a disadvantage, sir,' said Beardsley. 'I don't believe I know you?'

'Aw, but you do, Ben. As I said, it's been a long time. Ten years in fact. You've surely not forgotten those good ole days in Claxton County?'

Beardsley blanched. Recognition dawned in his cool blue eyes, and he looked less than happy at this unexpected reunion.

'Kane,' he said quietly. 'Norton Kane.'

'The same,' Kane continued to grin. He extended his hand. 'Put it there, pardner!' he said.

The other took Kane's hand, but without any great enthusiasm.

'How are you, Kane?' he asked.

'Jest fine, Ben. An' yo're lookin' pretty prosperous, I must say.'

'Yes. Wa'al, come on through. I gotta bottle of whiskey in my office. We oughta … er … celebrate this … er … chance encounter.' Beardsley smiled feebly and turned to his clerk. 'I'll leave you to mind the store, Andy,' he said.

'Sure thing, Mr Beardsley,' replied the youth.

Beardsley forced another smile and ushered Kane through into the office. However, once they were both seated in Beardsley's office and the door was closed behind them, the storekeeper rounded on his visitor.

'What in tarnation are you doin' here in Red Rock?' he demanded.

'Jest passin' through, is all.'

'That so?' The relief on Beardsley's face was unmistakable.

'Leastways, I was jest passin' through, but, now I've met you, Ben, reckon mebbe I'll stay on awhile.'

'Now, look here, Kane ….'

'No; you look here, Ben. You ain't got nuthin' on me, but I sure as hell have got somethin' on you.'

'Whaddya mean?'

'I mean that I know you spent seven years in Claxton County Jail for armed robbery.'

'Ssh, keep yore voice down!' hissed Beardsley, glancing fearfully towards his office door.

'Ah! So, you don't want yore clerk to know 'bout yore criminal past?'

'No, I do not.'

'Nor anybody else?'

'No.'

'That's what I figured. If'n the good folks of Red Rock were to discover that their mayor, that staunch, upright feller who married the preacher's daughter, was hidin' under a false name an' was in reality Ben Bradley, a convicted bank robber, they might be more'n jest a li'l upset. Folks don't like bein' deceived, an' they don't like smart bastards who pretend to be somethin' they ain't.'

'I changed my name, that's true,' replied Beardsley. 'But I certainly am not pretendin' to be somethin' I'm not. I paid my debt to society an', since I've been in Red Rock, I've lived a decent, honest life.'

'Quite the reformed character, huh?' sneered Kane.

'Yes. That's exactly what I am', said Beardsley.

'Still, you'd prefer that the folks hereabouts was kept in the dark 'bout yore past?'

'I've already said as much. T'aint no concern of theirs.'

'Not even of your wife?'

'You leave Jessica outa this.'

'Sure, Ben. I don't wanta cause no trouble 'tween man an' wife.' Kane smiled silkily and said in a conciliatory voice, 'Look, there ain't no reason for anybody to know 'bout yore past. You look after me an' I'll naturally keep my mouth shut.'

'Look after you?'

'Yeah. I've hit hard times, pardner, an' could do with a li'l financial assistance.'

'How much?'

'A coupla hundred dollars will do for now.'

'For now?'

'That's right. I'm figurin' on stayin' around awhile. So, when I need some more, I'll let you know.'

'I ain't made of money, Kane. I cain't ....'

'You can surely afford to bank-roll an ole pal who once saved yore life?'

'You never saved my life.'

'No, but that's the story I intend tellin' folks. We was out huntin' in the Big Horn Mountains an' I saved you from bein' killed by a bear. How will that do?'

Ben Beardsley scowled. He knew he had little choice other than to go along with Norton Kane's plan. The idea of Jessica and her parents finding out that he had been to prison appalled him. He knew he should have confided in them before he and Jessica married, but he had been afraid that, if he did, he would lose her. Now, with the arrival in Red Rock of his old cell-mate, he wished he had made a clean breast of it. He swore beneath his breath. His marriage was under threat, as was his position as town mayor. There was an election due in the fall and who would vote for a once-time bank robber? If Kane opened his mouth, he, Beardsley, could lose everything he held dear, his wife, his children, and his standing in the community. He would still have his businesses, but what would be the point of running them if he was abandoned by wife and children and treated as a pariah by his fellow-citizens? This might not happen, of course, yet it could all too easily, and it was a risk he dared not take. He would have to buy Kane's silence.

'Okay,' he said. 'I s'pose yore story would account for you an' me being' acquainted. How long are you proposin' to stay in town, anyways?'

'I dunno. I've been ridin' hard an' long these last few weeks. Guess I could do with restin' up awhile.'

'I see.'

'So, how's about handin' over them coupla hundred dollars we spoke of?'

'You spoke of.' Beardsley continued to scowl, but, nevertheless, he went over to his safe and began to fiddle with the combination. Then he threw open the heavy steel door and extracted a large wad of notes. He counted out two hundred dollars, returned the rest of the wad to the safe and closed the door. 'Here you are, Kane,' he said.

Kane grinned widely, as he accepted the roll of dollar bills.

'That's mighty generous of you, pardner,' he said.

'Yeah, wa'al, I expect that, in return, you'll keep yore trap shut,' said Beardsley.

''Course. Ten years ago, we once hunted together an' I saved yore life. That's the story, huh?'

'Yes. That's the story.'

'Okay, guess I'll take that glass of whiskey now that our business is settled,' said Kane.

Beardsley nodded. He had forgotten the excuse for closeting his visitor in the office had been so that he might offer him a glass of whiskey.

Beardsley produced the bottle from a cupboard above his writing desk and poured two generous measures. He eyed the amber liquid avidly. He badly needed a drink.

TWO

Red Rock boasted two saloons, one hotel and three or four rooming-houses. The hotel was rather inappropriately named the Grand. A two-storey, white-painted frame building, it was adequate, but no more than that. Still, it was the best Red Rock had to offer and Norton Kane cheerfully took a room there. He had his sorrel taken care of at Ben Beardsley's livery stables and that evening he enjoyed himself at the Golden Garter. Unlike Flanagan's Saloon, it was not simply a saloon. It was also a bordello and a gambling joint. Roulette and his girls between them earned the proprietor, Dan Evans, a comfortable living, particularly when the cowboys from the nearby Bar Q and Lazy S ranches rode into town. Saturday nights at the Golden Garter were apt to be pretty wild. Mid-week, on the other hand, was very quiet and Kane had the pick of Dan Evans' girls. He chose a plump little bottle-blonde called Kitty and had no reason to regret his choice. She gave him the best time he had had in months.

On the following morning, Kane visited the

town's dry goods store and purchased a whole new
rig-out, from low-crowned Stetson right down to
shiny leather boots, all in black. His old clothes he
left with the owner of the dry goods store, to
dispose of as he liked. That done, Kane headed for
Flanagan's Saloon, where he spent the rest of the
morning playing poker and drinking Flanagan's
most expensive whiskey. A slap-up lunch at the
Grand Hotel was followed by more of the same,
while dinner at the hotel preceded another visit to
the Golden Garter, a session at the roulette wheel
and a further romp in bed with the voluptuous
Kitty.

In this manner, Norton Kane proceeded to pass
his days and nights at Red Rock. And, naturally
enough, he had, from time to time, to return to
Ben Beardsley for more money to spend. Dan
Evans, his croupier Rick Grainger, and the girls of
the Golden Garter were all delighted to entertain
so free-spending a customer, but Frank Flanagan,
although he took the man in black's money,
continued to regard him with deep suspicion.

Another person to regard Kane with deep
suspicion was Luke Tanner. Tanner had been
sheriff of Red Rock for more years than he cared to
remember. Now in his late fifties, a short,
thick-set fellow with grizzled hair beneth his grey
Stetson, shrewd brown eyes and a weathered,
rather heavily-lined face, he was nobody's fool. No
longer as quick on the draw as once he had been,
Tanner relied heavily on his experience and
common sense to keep the peace in Red Rock.

Also, in the last couple of years, he had been aided and abetted by a young deputy, whom he was training to succeed him.

Johnnie Reid was a tall, gangling youth with ingenuous blue eyes and a frank, open countenance. He was honest and he was keen to do his duty. In addition, despite his gangling looks, he was no slouch with a gun. Like the sheriff, Johnnie Reid wore a Colt Peacemaker tied down on his right thigh, and on Saturday nights, when the cowboys were in town, he carried a scatter-gun on his evening rounds. Between them, the sheriff and his deputy combined to ensure Red Rock remained pretty peaceful. Both men wanted to keep things that way. Therefore, neither was particularly happy at Norton Kane's decision to stay on in town.

On the fifth morning of Kane's visit, they watched him leave the Grand Hotel, cross Main Street and make his way as usual to Flanagan's.

'Why don't you tell him to mosey on outa town?' asked Johnnie Reid.

'I'd sure like to, Johnnie,' replied Tanner. 'But I got no reason. He ain't done nuthin' I can hold agin' him.'

'Yet I can tell you don't trust him. You reckon he's gonna cause us a whole heap of trouble, don't yuh?'

'Yeah. I know the kind. He's like a drowsin' rattlesnake. Sometime or other, he'll rouse hisself an' then he'll strike.'

'D'you reckon he's a feller with a price on his head?'

'Could be. But he ain't wanted in this here state. I checked.'

'Oh!'

'So, we're stuck with him, I guess.'

'Mebbe he'll grow tired of Red Rock an' move on of his own accord?'

'Not while Ben Beardsley's bank-rollin' him, he won't.'

Johnnie Reid whistled.

'You know that for a fact?' he asked.

Luke Tanner frowned and shook his head.

'Nope; I'm simply guessin'. But it figures. This feller Kane rides into town lookin' like some goddam saddle tramp, then he recognises our mayor an' goes over an' introduces hisself. Seems, 'bout ten years back, he saved Ben's life. Next thing, Kane's stayin' at the Grand, has purchased a whole new set of expensive clothin' an' is spendin' money at the Golden Garter an' Flanagan's like there's no tomorrow. Now, the question is, did he bring that kinda dough with him?'

'I wouldn't have thought so, Sheriff.'

'Me neither, Johnnie. No, I reckon he's spendin' Ben's money all right.'

'Wa'al, if'n he did save Mr Beardsley's life. ...'

'Yeah, I guess Ben'd figure he owed him.' Tanner sighed. He liked and admired the mayor, and he could fully understand Beardsley's readiness to help out an old friend, particularly an old friend who had once saved his life. But, if that was the case, why had Beardsley not invited Kane to his home, to meet his wife and children? And why, since Kane had been in town, had Beardsley never once joined him for a few friendly drinks at either Flanagan's or the Golden Garter? 'There's somethin' that jest ain't right!' he concluded.

The sheriff was not the only one to consider Beardsley's failure to invite his old friend home rather surprising. Beardsley's wife also deemed it strange. And so it was that, much against his better judgment, Beardsley invited Norton Kane to his home for Sunday lunch. Also invited were Jessica's parents, the Reverend John Dwyer and his wife, Rachel. The meal was not, however, a great success. Norton Kane felt and looked ill-at-ease and the conversation flagged. Consequently, Jessica did not press her husband to repeat the invitation, much to both Beardsley's and Kane's relief. From then onwards, Beardsley encountered Kane only on those occasions when the gunslinger visited him, at one or other of his business establishments, to extort some more money.

And so the days passed into weeks, and Norton Kane quickly became the most popular customer the Golden Garter had ever had. He gambled recklessly and, when he won, which he did now and then, he invariably handed the croupier, Rick Grainger, a generous tip. He was equally generous to Dan Evans' girls, all of whom he bedded at one time or another. The voluptuous bottle-blonde, Kitty, remained his favourite, though, for she was by far and away the most inventive and exciting of Dan Evans' whores. Indeed, it was his craving for Kitty's favours that eventually brought about Kane's downfall.

He had been nearly five weeks at Red Rock and had got into the habit of visiting the Golden Garter most evenings. Saturdays, however, were an exception. On that particular night of the week, the ranch hands from the Bar Q and the Lazy S swarmed into the bordello and kept the girls pretty busy. Kane, therefore, left them to it. He had no wish to queue up for his turn, not when, for the rest of the week, he could have whichever girl he fancied for as long as he fancied. Instead, he would spend his Saturday nights at Flanagan's, playing poker with some of the townsfolk and with those among the cowboys, the older, quieter element, who preferred gambling to fornicating.   It was unfortunate, therefore, that on the late afternoon of Kane's fifth Saturday in Red Rock, he encountered Kitty on the sidewalk outside his hotel. The previous two nights he had spent twenty miles away in Plainville, where he had gone for a short change of scenery. The visit had not been altogether successful, though, for he had found the town incredibly dull. He was glad to be back in Red Rock and was in just the mood to yield to Kitty's ample charms.

'Howdy, Norton, where have you been these last coupla evenin's? Me an' the girls, we sure missed you,' said the blonde, bestowing upon him her most seductive smile.

Kane eyed the girl up and down. He noted

Kitty's pretty, saucy features, her wide, generous mouth, the soft white arms and the full, ripe breasts pushing up from the bodice of her dark-red velvet dress. He felt his blood beginning to race.

'I've been over to Plainville,' he said.

'There ain't much doin' there.'

'Nope.' Kane smiled. 'I was jest steppin' across to Flanagan's. Care to join me?' he asked.

'For a drink?'

'That was the general idea, Kitty.'

'We sell liquor at the Golden Garter.'

'I tend to leave the Golden Garter to the cowboys on Saturday nights.'

'I had noticed. But it's early yet. The boys from the Bar Q an' the Lazy S won't hit town for an hour or more.'

Kane considered. This was true. He was sorely tempted. He stared the girl straight in the eye. Her dark brown orbs were warm and oh so inviting.

'Okay,' he said. 'We'll celebraate my return by crackin' a bottle of champagne in yore room.'

Norton Kane knew that Dan Evans' 'champagne' bore little or no resemblance to the real stuff. But Kitty seemed to like it and, anyway, Evans expected her and the other girls to promote it. So, Kane invariably played along and ordered it. Why should he care? He was buying it with Ben Beardsley's money.

He linked arms with the blonde, and they turned and headed along the sidewalk towards the Golden Garter.

The next three hours passed very pleasantly

indeed. Kane had intended spending only one of them in bed with Kitty, for he planned to join the big Saturday night poker game at Flanagan's, a game which attracted the ranch owners, Jim Pelham from the Bar Q and Les Gates from the Lazy S, Doc Brady the town's physician, Felix Oates its mortician, and a number of Red Rock's other prominent citizens.

In the event, however, he was still with Kitty at the end of those three hours. By this time, he had had his fill of fornication and was looking forward to sitting in on the poker game at Flanagan's. He dressed with his customary care, watched from the bed by the still-naked Kitty. She had enjoyed her session with Kane. Although a professional whore, Kitty took pleasure from her work, at least with some of her clients. She was not looking forward, though, to the remainder of the evening, for the cowboys in the main were a rough and ready bunch and by no means the most considerate or satisfying of bedfellows.

It was as Kane strapped on his gun-belt and bent to tie the holster down to his right thigh that the first knock sounded upon Kitty's bedroom door. This was followed by a regular hammering and then by demands in a loud, drunken voice that the door be opened pronto ... or else. Kane scowled and, stepping briskly across the room, threw open the door. He found himself confronted by a large, broad-shouldered cowpoke. The cowpoke was clearly very drunk and also very young. Although six foot four inches in his stockinged feet and solidly built, he had the pink-cheeked, youthful countenance of a seventeen or eighteen year old.

'Whaddya want?' snarled Kane.

The young cowboy grinned.

'I want Kitty,' he said.

'You could've waited till I'd finished,' rasped Kane.

'I've been waitin' for more'n an hour.

'There are other girls you could've had.'

'I didn't want no other girls. I wanted Kitty.'

'That's nice,' said Kitty, sitting up in bed and affording the youth an excellent view of her superb young breasts.

Inflamed by the sight of Kitty's naked torso, the youth lunged forward and attempted to push past Kane. But the gunslinger stood firm and blocked the other's passage.

'Not so fast!' he hissed.

'Git outa my way!' cried the cowboy. 'It's clear you've finished yore business here an' so. ...'

'You didn't know that when you started hammerin' on that there door,' snapped Kane.

'Nope. But I reckoned you'd had long enough.'

'Yeah, wa'al, that's surely up to me? I don't need no stupid kid to tell me when my time is up.'

'I ain't stupid, an' I ain't no kid!' retorted the youth angrily.

'Nope?' Kane's eyes glittered venomously, his right hand hovering above the butt of his Colt Peacemaker. 'Then let's see what kinda man you really are,' he sneered.

'He ain't carryin' no gun, Norton!' cried Kitty, alarmed at the sudden turn of events and anxious that the matter should be resolved peaceably.

Although flattered by the idea of the pair wanting to fight over her, she had no wish that they should resort to gun-play. To this end she was joined by the youth's fellow ranch-hands, a number of whom had been attracted by all the hammering and shouting. They were by now bunched together in Kitty's doorway.

'That's right, dude!' yelled one of them. 'Bobby ain't got no gun. Hell, none of us have! You oughta know that!'

Kane grimaced. He had forgotten the town ordinance forbidding the hands of the Bar Q and Lazy S ranches from carrying any kind of firearm within the town limits. This had been introduced some years earlier following a drunken brawl between hands from the two ranches, a brawl in which four of them were shot and badly wounded. The idea had been Sheriff Luke Tanner's; it had been approved by the town council and reluctantly accepted by the two ranch owners. Since then, the worst anyone had suffered was a broken nose or a black eye, and both Jim Pelham and Les Gates had subsequently agreed that the ordinance was an excellent thing. Their men might still grumble at having to unstrap their gun-belts prior to riding into Red Rock, but the ranchers recognised all too clearly the benefits of the new law. It also made life a whole heap easier for its originator, the sheriff.

'What's goin' on?' cried another voice from the rear of the crowd milling in and around the doorway.

'Bobby McCoy an' that dude Kane are spoilin' for a fight.'

'Yippee! There ain't nuthin' like a good fist-fight!' yelled the newcomer.

'Sure ain't! You show the dude, Bobby, that he cain't tangle with us boys from the Bar Q!'

'Wa'al, let's not disappoint 'em,' grinned the youth.

'Whaddya mean?'

Kane glanced uneasily about him. He was a gunman, not a pugilist, and he had not the slightest desire to swap punches with the young giant confronting him.

'I mean, if'n you wanta see what kinda man I am, yo're gonna have to take off yore gun-belt an' step outside onto the sidewalk,' said Bobby McCoy.

This statement was greeted by loud cheers. Only Kane and Kitty looked less than exultant.

'I don't think there's any need for a fight,' began the girl.

'You keep outa this, Kitty,' snapped Bobby McCoy. Then he turned to face Kane and, grinning widely, enquired, 'You comin', Mr Kane, or are you jest plumb yeller?'

Kane cursed beneath his breath. He had talked himself into a fight he had no chance of winning. He ought to have noticed that McCoy wasn't carrying a gun. Indeed, he ought to have remembered Red Rock's gun law. Shooting down the young lunkhead was one thing; fighting him with bare fists was quite another. But he had no choice. Reluctantly, he began to unbuckle his gun-belt.

'I'm comin',' he said quietly.

Kane tossed his gun onto Kitty's bed and instructed the girl to take care of it for him. Then he and Bobby McCoy and the other cowboys hurried off downstairs. They rushed across the bar-room of the Golden Garter towards the batwing doors. These were promptly thrust open and the crowd poured outside, whereupon a ring of bodies was formed in the street, at the foot of the steps leading up to the saloon. It was a large ring and was illuminated by the lights thrown from the doorway and windows of the Golden Garter. Into its centre stepped Bobby McCoy. He removed his check shirt to display a powerful, well-muscled upper body. Kane followed him into the ring. The gunslinger discarded his black leather vest, but contented himself with merely rolling up the sleeves of his black shirt. Both combatants had previously removed their hats.

'Now we'll see who's the better man,' said Bobby McCoy cheerfully.

'You bet!' cried one of his pals.

The two men circled each other. Kane eyed the other warily. He held up his fists in front of his face, waiting for the other to make the first move so that he might counter-attack. He did not have long to wait. Bobby McCoy suddenly darted forward and lashed out with a long, swinging right hand. It was something of a haymaker and Kane was easily able to duck beneath it. But he had not reckoned on the speed with which McCoy would follow up with a left hook. Kane ducked under the right hand and straight into the left. The blow struck him beneath the chin and lifted him clean off his feet. He hit the dusty street with a sickening thud and lay there for a few moments, the breath knocked out of his body and his brain spinning.

Slowly, painfully, Kane scrambled to his feet. He spat out a mouthful of blood, his tongue running over his teeth, some of which the punch had loosened. He rushed forward in a crouching run, jabbing with both hands. His first punch caught McCoy beneath the heart. His second failed to connect, another left hook from the cowboy penetrated Kane's guard and thudded into his belly. The gunslinger gasped and doubled up. As he did so, Bobby McCoy belted him with two tremendous blows to the face. One split his upper lip, while the other smashed his nose into a bloody pulp. Once again Norton Kane hit the dusty street with a sickening thud.

The crowd were baying delightedly. They had come to see their man give the stranger a beating and he was doing just that. Kane's aura of menace had not gone unremarked by the cowboys. Like Red Rock's townsfolk, they had viewed him with distinct unease. But now he was reduced to a battered, bloodied, moaning hulk, they no longer

feared him. Rapturously, they cheered Bobby
McCoy as he continued to dish out further
punishment to his hapless opponent.

Four times Norton Kane was knocked down.
Four times he managed to stagger to his feet.
However, before Bobby McCoy could recommence
his assault upon the gunslinger for a fifth time, a
short, thick-set figure forced his way through the
crowd and into the ring. He stepped between the
two protagonists.

'Okay, fellers,' he said. 'Enough is enough. The
fight's over.'

The crowd protested, but Sheriff Luke Tanner
was adamant. He and his deputy had been about
to commence their evening rounds when the
Reverend John Dwyer had called to inform them
that a fight was taking place outside the Golden
Garter. Had Tanner known that Kane was
involved and was losing, he might well have
delayed his arrival upon the scene. But now he
was there, he felt obliged to uphold the law.
Besides, he could see that Kane had already taken
a pretty bad beating.

'You heard what the sheriff said,' yelled
Johnnie Reid.

The youngster covered the crowd with his
scatter-gun while Tanner helped the unfortunate
gunslinger to stagger off up the street to the law
office.

In point of fact, the crowd was reasonably
satisfied. Kane hadn't been knocked senseless,
but he had been thoroughly beaten, and there was

no doubt that the honour of the Bar Q ranch had been upheld. Consequently, they soon began to disperse, the majority hurrying up the steps onto the sidewalk and then back into the saloon. Among their number was the hero of the evening, a flushed and triumphant Bobby McCoy.

He did not bother to pull on his shirt. Carrying it over one arm, he straightaway made his way upstairs to Kitty's room. The blonde had watched the fight from her window and was expecting him. She was secretly pleased that the youngster had waited over an hour for her services, rather than settle for those of another of Dan Evans' girls. Also, the sight of the two men fighting had aroused her sexually. As a result, she was as anxious for Bobby McCoy's embraces as he was for hers.

Upon his entering the room, Kitty drew the curtains to and turned to face him. His naked torso had perspired during the course of the fight and now it glistened in the light of the kerosene lamp. Kitty eyed it avidly and shrugged off the lacy black negligee, which she had worn while standing at the window. A quotation she had once heard suddenly sprang to mind.

'To the victor the spoils,' she said huskily.

THREE

Norton Kane passed out and had to be carried by the sheriff and his deputy the last few yards to the law office. When he came to, he found himself slumped in the sheriff's armchair with Doc Brady and the sheriff leaning over him. Johnnie Reid had belatedly commenced his evening rounds and was gone.

'Wa'al, Mr Kane, you sure have taken one helluva beating,' said the docter.

'I don't need you to tell me that, Doc,' groaned Kane.

'Nope. Guess you don't at that.' Doc Brady, a large, fat, florid-faced fellow, pushed his brown Derby to the back of his head and smiled. 'You'll be glad to hear, though, that you've suffered no serious injury. A broken nose, a black eye an' a coupla cracked ribs, an ' that's about it,' he said cheerily .

Kane felt a deal less sanguine about this catalogue of injuries. The nose, in particular, bothered him. He knew it was mangled pretty badly and the pain from it made him wince.

'My nose,' he mumbled.'That's all smashed up. I cain't scarcely breathe out of it.'

'It looks worse 'n it is. Guess it's broke in a coupla places, but, when the swellin' goes down, it'll be okay. A mite squint, mebbe. Still, that ain't nuthin' to worry 'bout,' said Doc Brady airily.

Kane's one good eye glared angrily at the doctor. Brady's cavalier attitude riled him. Kane glanced from the doctor to the sheriff.

'Wa'al Sheriff, whaddya propose doin'?' he demanded.

'Nuthin',' said the lawman.

'Nuthin'? You allow young punks like that lunkhead McCoy to beat up innocent citizens, do yuh?' rasped Kane

Luke Tanner grinned broadly.

'It was a fair fight,' he said. ''Sides, you ain't what I'd exactly call an innocent citizen.'

'Whaddya mean by that?'

'I mean, Mr Kane, that I know yore kind. You may not be a wanted man in this state, but I figure there's states where the law's mighty keen to catch up with you.'

'You don't know that for sure.'

'Nope. Which is why I cain't run you outa town.'

'Is that the only reason? Ain't you forgettin' I'm a partickler pal of yore mayor?'

'Are you now? He owes you, I'll grant you that. But he don't seem so all-fired fond of you. Anyways, I'm the law around here an' I'm the one who decides who goes an' who stays.'

Kane felt a violent rage swell up inside him.

Who the hell did Tanner think he was? For two pins he would plug the sheriff and damn the consequences. Then he remembered that he had left his gun in Kitty's safe-keeping. Therefore, he forced himself to calm down. Presently sanity prevailed, and he realised that he was in no condition to do anything other than retire to bed.

'Yeah, wa'al I ain't quittin' Red Rock till I'm good an' ready,' he said defiantly. 'An' now, if one of you two'll help me outa this chair, I'll mosey on back to my hotel.'

Between them, Tanner and Doc Brady lifted the gunslinger out of the depths of the armchair. The doctor then took it upon himself to help Kane stagger the short distance to the Grand Hotel. He half-carried the battered, still groggy gunman upstairs to his room and laid him down on his bed. And there he left him.

The next morning Norton Kane examined his battered, bloodied features in the cracked, fly-blown bedroom mirror. He did not like what he saw, for he was not a pretty sight. He felt angry and humiliated that he, one of the West's most notorious gunslingers, should have allowed himself to be trapped into a fist-fight and then ignominiously beaten by a teenaged youth. He had his pride and it had been very badly dented.

Consequently, Kane determined not to show his face until it was healed. Even then, he thought ruefully, the broken nose would bear testimony to his devastating defeat at the hands of the cowboy.

He cursed loud and long. Maybe he should have rested up at Red Rock for no more than a few days, then squeezed as much money as he could out of Ben Beardsley and ridden on? He cursed some more. But chewing over what he might have done was quite pointless. A look of sheer venom flooded the bruised and bloodied features of his thin face. He decided there and then that he would have his revenge and then ride out of Red Rock, never to return.

Kane arranged that the hotel should bring his meals to his room until further notice. And there he stayed, nursing his wounds and his wrath, and plotting vengeance against Bobby McCoy.

However, he was not forgotten. Kitty, accompanied by Dan Evans, called at the hotel on the morning after the fight, anxious to show sympathy towards the man who, since his arrival in Red Rock, had become the Golden Garter's most valued customer. But Kane would not see them. Therefore, all Kitty could do was hand Kane's gun to the hotel clerk, with instructions that he should return it to its owner, and then retrace her steps to the Golden Garter.

It was not until the fourth day after his beating that he admitted his first visitor, Rick Grainger. The croupier was a small, foxy-faced man with shifty eyes and thinning black hair, plastered damply across an egg-like dome. Kane eyed him closely. During the period he had remained in quiet isolation in his hotel room, the gunman had devised a plan to wreak his vengeance upon the youngster who had humiliated him. However, in order to carry through this plan, he needed an accomplice, and he reckoned that Rick Grainger could be just the man. He had already divined that Grainger was greedy for money and unlikely to be earning very much from Dan Evans. Why the croupier was working in the Golden Garter and not in one of the big casinos or saloons in Dodge City or Wichita, Kane could only guess. But, whatever the reason, he figured it had to be to the man's discredit, for Grainger was competent enough at his job.

'Come on in,' he said, summoning up a welcoming smile.

Grainger stepped inside the small, sparsely-furnished bedroom. Still smiling, Kane ushered him onto one of the two rather rickety chairs available, and offered him a slug of red-eye. Then, once he had dispensed the whiskey, Kane settled himself upon the other chair.

'To yore good health, Mr Kane!' said Grainger. 'I'd've come before only Mr Evans told me you weren't receivin' visitors.'

'Nope. I didn't want folks to see me the way I was,' replied the gunslinger.

'I s'pose not.'

Grainger averted his eyes and stared down at his drink. His host's face was still showing distinct signs of his recent beating. The swelling over his left eye had gone down, but the area round it was still badly discoloured. There were other bruises, too, and the split lip, although

healing fast, remained all too visible. As for
Kane's nose, it was no longer swollen, but it
looked very painful, being almost black in colour
and clearly misshapen.

'I realise I still ain't exactly pretty to look at,'
said Kane wryly. 'But the bruises are at least
beginnin' to fade.'

'So, you'll soon be visitin' us again at the Golden
Garter?' said Grainger.

'Not until 'bout the middle of next week, I
reckon.'

'You plannin' to stay cooped up here till then?'

'Yup.'

'That's gonna git mighty borin'.'

'It already is. But you can send Kitty along 'fore
then. In a coupla days, say. I guess I need the
exercise.'

Rick Grainger grinned.

'Anythin' else I can git you?' he asked.

This time it was Kane's turn to grin.

'Yeah, now you mention it, there is,' he said.

'Name it.'

'A hand-gun, complete with holster an' gun-
belt.'

Grainger's eyes widened in surprise. He looked
across at Kane's bed. The gunman's Colt
Peacemaker was hanging there in its holster, the
gun-belt fastened round one of the bedposts.

'You already got....' he began.

'I know what I've already got,' snapped Kane.

'So, why d'you need another hand-gun?'
enquired the croupier curiously.

'That's my business.'

Grainger caught the malignant stare directed at him by his host. Once again, he glanced down at his drink, and then nervously muttered, 'Yeah. 'Course it is, Mr Kane.'

'So, will you git me what I've asked for?'

'Sure, Mr Kane. I'll mosey on over to Ben Beardsley's store an'. ...'

'Nope.'

'Nope?'

'You do that an' all Red Rock will know I've bought me a hand-gun. You know how gossip spreads in a small town.'

'So what? Why shouldn't folks know?'

''Cause it's my business, is why.'

'Wa'al. ...'

'You known in Plainville?'

'Guess not. I've only been there a coupla times. A dull kinda place. It's got more saloons'n Red Rock, but none quite like the Golden Garter.'

'No?'

'Nope. They ain't none of 'em got either girls or a roulette wheel.'

'All the same, I'd like you to take a ride over there.'

'But Plainville's at least twenty miles away!'

'So, you could git there an' back in a day.'

'Yeah, but. ...'

'Don't you wanta do me this favour?'

''Course I do, Mr Kane. Only. ...'

'There's twenty dollars in it for you.'

Grainger's eyes glittered greedily. Yet still he

hesitated.

'Twenty. Hmm; I dunno?'

'Twenty-five, an' that's my last offer.'

There was a note of finality in Kane's voice. Grainger shrugged his thin shoulders and smiled weakly.

'Okay, Mr Kane. I'll ride over to Plainville tomorrow.'

'Fine.' Kane pulled a small wad of dollar bills from his vest pocket and peeled off a few of the notes. He handed them to the croupier. 'There, that should cover the cost of the gun,' he said.

'Er ... what about my twenty-five dollars?' mumbled Grainger.

'You'll git 'em when I git the gun.'

'Ah!'

'An', Rick, this li'l transaction is a secret 'tween you an' me, okay? You don't tell anyone; not Dan Evans, not Kitty, not nobody.'

Grainger nodded. It was a complete mystery to him why Norton Kane should want to purchase a second gun. And why he should want to keep it a secret was an even bigger mystery. But that, as far as Grainger was concerned, was Kane's business. He was certainly curious, but he rather suspected that it was best if he did not know.

'I won't tell nobody, an' I'll make sure nobody sees me smugglin' the gun up here to yore room,' he promised.

'That's a good feller,' said Kane, smiling, and he lifted the whiskey bottle and offered to replenish his guest's tumbler.

* * *

The next person to visit Kane in his bedroom was the town mayor. He came mid-way through the morning, on the day following the croupier's visit.

Kane greeted his old cell-mate with some asperity.

'You took yore time comin',' he said acidly.

'I heard you weren't receivin' visitors.'

'So, what brought you along today?'

'I was told Rick Grainger called yesterday an' stayed for about an hour, so I thought I'd drop in an' see how you were.'

'Wa'al, as you can see, I'm on the mend.'

'Yeah.' Beardsley looked the other straight in the eye and said quietly, 'Red Rock ain't yore kinda town, Kane. Don't you reckon it's time you moved on?'

Much to his surprise, Kane nodded and replied, 'Jest what I was thinkin' myself, Ben. Once the bruisin' is all gone an' I'm lookin' presentable agin, guess I'll lam outa this one-horse town.'

Beardsley could not help but look relieved. He commented with some feeling, 'A wise move, if I may say so.'

'Naturally you may, though I'll expect a li'l farewell gift from the ole buddy whose life I once saved,' said Kane.

Beardsley's features tightened and his eyes narrowed.

'What kinda li'l gift have you in mind?' he asked anxiously.

'Oh, jest a small donation to help me on my way.'

'How small?'

'One thousand dollars.'

'Yo're crazy!'

'Am I? Yo're a wealthy man, Ben. Surely it's worth a thousand dollars to see me gone an' yore guilty secret safe once more?'

'Mebbe. But I ain't that rich. You've been bleedin' me regularly over the last few weeks, spendin' my hard-earned money on gamblin', an' drinkin', an' those painted trollops at the Golden Garter. Wa'al, my resources ain't inexhaustible. Most of my cash is tied up in my businesses, in my stock an'. ...'

'One thousand dollars. I ain't wranglin' with you, Ben.'

'In that case, you'd best open the window an' tell the world what you know.'

Kane stared at the tall, broad-shouldered figure of the reformed bank robber. He could see that Beardsley was not bluffing. The colour had left the mayor's cheeks, and he stood there, trembling with anger and clenching and unclenching his fists.

'How much can you afford?' asked Kane softly.

'Five hundred. No more.'

'Okay. You git it an' keep hold of it till I ask for it.'

'An' when is that likely to be?'

'When I'm ready to leave town.'

'You needn't wait till all the bruisin's gone. You could always leave under cover of darkness.'

'I ain't sneakin' away from Red Rock like some thief in the night. No sirree, when I leave, I ride out with my head held high!' declared Kane.

'But. ...'

'My mind's made up, Ben. You'll jest have to be patient a mite longer.'

Beardsley nodded. The fact that Norton Kane was actually planning to leave town had cheered him enormously. Also, he could use a few days to gather together his parting gift to the outlaw. And the main thing was that the end of his ordeal was in sight. Leastways, that was what he thought.

During the days following the mayor's visit, Kane's looks continued to improve, and he whiled away the time quite pleasantly in the company of Kitty and the rest of the girls from the Golden Garter, one or other of whom he entertained in his hotel room on seccessive afternoons. His only other visitors were Ben Beardsley and Rick Grainger. The former called to inform Kane that he had the five hundred dollars ready for him to collect whenever he wished, while the latter called to hand over an Army Model Colt revolver and its accoutrements.

Kane carefully examined and loaded the colt. He smiled. His plan was complete. All he had to do now was wait. It was early on a Thursday evening when Grainger smuggled the gun up to his room. Two days to go. He hid the gun, the holster and the gun-belt in one of his saddle-bags. For his plan to succeed, it was vital that nobody should know he possessed the Army Model Colt.

The hands from the Bar Q and Lazy S ranches hit

town as usual on that Saturday night. Among
them was Bobby McCoy. It was now two weeks
since his fist-fight with the man in black, and he
had almost forgotten the incident. He followed his
usual routine. He hitched his gelding outside
Flanagan's Saloon and went in with his foreman,
Ned Baines, and a couple of the Bar Q's older
hands. They enjoyed a few quiet drinks together
and then, when the older three adjourned from
the bar to a nearby poker game, McCoy left the
saloon and headed down Main Street towards the
Golden Garter. There he proposed to meet up with
the remainder of the Bar Q hands and drink,
gamble and fornicate the night away. He could not
make up his mind whether he would sample the
lovely Kitty's ample charms or those of Dan
Evans' latest acquisition, a small, slender redhead with a face like that of a Botticelli angel.

Bobby McCoy was debating this in his mind and
wondering whether, over the course of the night,
he might perhaps succeed in bedding both young
women, when he found himself approaching the
corner of South and Main Streets. The Golden
Garter stood about a couple of hundred yards
away, on the opposite side of Main Street. McCoy
paused at the top of the steps leading down from
the sidewalk, and gave a loud belch. As he did so,
a black-clad figure glided silently out of the
shadow of Art Bush's shuttered dry goods store
and stepped swiftly up behind him. McCoy gasped
as he suddenly felt the muzzle of a gun jab hard
into his ribs.

'What the hell...?' he began.

'Shuddup!' Norton Kane hissed in his ear.

'But, I don't. ...'

'You do exactly as yo're told, or I'll blast a hole in you so big you could ram yore fist into it,' snarled the gunman.

'Okay ... okay, jest take it easy, pal!' stammered the cowboy nervously.

'Right, then. Head on down them steps an' then turn an' make yore way slowly along South Street,' said Kane.

'Sure ... sure thing.'

Bobby McCoy did as he was bid, and the two men proceeded along South Street for approximately one hundred yards. There was nobody about, for there was nothing in South Street to attract anyone at that hour. Livery stables, a feed and grain store, a blacksmith's forge, a funeral parlour and the rail depot, all were deserted and would be until the following morning.

'Okay, McCoy, that's far enough.'

Bobby McCoy halted.

'What now?' he asked.

'You can turn round an' face me,' said Kane.

Slowly, hesitantly, Bobby McCoy turned round. He had guessed that his assailant was the gunslinger.

'What's the big idea, Kane?' he demanded.

'It's quite simple,' replied Kane coldly. 'You humiliated me, an' that's somethin' I don't forgive. Ever. So, I'm gonna have to kill you.'

'Are you crazy or somethin'? You shoot me an'

you'll hang for sure!' exclaimed the youngster.

'Is that a fact?'

'Yes, it it. You cain't shoot an unarmed man an' hope to git away with it.'

'That's where yo're wrong, sonny.'

Kane smiled grimly and aimed the Colt Peacemaker, which he was holding in his right hand, at the young man's heart. His eyes gleamed malevolently as he squeezed the trigger. The forty-five calibre slug struck Bobby McCoy in the chest, smashing through muscle and bone and exiting out of his back in a gush of crimson blood. The second shot hit him in the forehead as he fell backwards. It exploded inside his skull, blasting his brains out and killing him instantly.

Immediately, Norton Kane dashed forward. Over his left shoulder were draped a gun-belt and holster. He returned the Colt Peacemaker to its holster and removed the revolver from the one attached to the superfluous gun-belt. Then, aiming skywards, he fired a single shot.

This done, Kane quickly stooped down and, lifting the dead cowboy, slipped the gun-belt beneath him and round his waist. He then fastened the belt and hastily tied down the holster to Bobby McCoy's right thigh. Thereupon, he placed the still-smoking gun into the youngster's right hand.

All of this was accomplished in but a few seconds. Kane glanced anxiously over his shoulder. The street remained deserted. And so, smiling triumphantly, he rose to his feet and stepped back a few paces, where he stood staring down at the lifeless body of his victim.

Such was the scene which greeted Sheriff Luke Tanner and his deputy, when they, together with a number of others who had heard the shots, came running into South Street.

Tanner glanced from Kane to the still, prostrate body of Bobby McCoy. The sheriff's face suffused with righteous indignation and he roared, 'Goddammit, Kane, you've gone an' murdered the boy!'

Kane shook his head.

'No, Sheriff,' he said. 'It was a fair fight. McCoy fired once an' missed, while I fired twice an' hit him both times.'

Johnnie Reid, who had dropped onto his knees beside the dead cowboy, carefully examined the Army Model Colt and sniffed at the revolver's muzzle. He glanced unhappily up at his superior.

'Kane's right, Sheriff,' he said. 'This here gun's been fired all right.'

Tanner scowled darkly and exclaimed, 'But, hell, there's a law agin' cowpokes from the Bar Q carryin' firearms within the town limits!'

'That's right. An', when we rode into Red Rock, Bobby wasn't carryin' no gun,' said Ned Baines, who, upon hearing the shots, had promptly abandoned his poker game at Flanagan's Saloon and hurried to see what was happening.

'Wa'al, he's carryin' a gun now. You can see for yoreself,' said Kane.

'That's so,' said Tanner.

'It don't make no sense,' said Baines. 'Why in tarnation would he wanta carry a gun? He never did before.'

'We'd have noticed if he'd been wearin' one when we rode into town,' said another of the Bar Q's hands.

'Yeah; an' I'd swear he wasn't,' stated another.

'Swear what you like. Seein' is believin',' said Kane. He turned to the sheriff. 'Is it okay with you, Sheriff,' he asked, 'if I mosey on back to my hotel? All this excitement has made me feel a mite weary.'

Tanner bit his lip. He knew something wasn't right. But he also knew he couldn't prove it.

'Guess so,' he growled grudgingly.

'Say, Sheriff, ain't you gonna arrest the sonofabitch?' cried Baines.

'On what charge?' asked Tanner.

'On a charge of murder, of course.'

'But, if 'n' it was a fair fight …!'

'It sure as hell wasn't!'

Kane laughed harshly.

'Can you prove that?' he sneered.

'Reckon I can at that,' said the Bar Q foreman, staring fixedly at the still, spreadeagled figure of the young cowboy.

Ned Baines was not the most observant of men, and it had passed his notice when he had first glanced at Bobby McCoy's cadaver. Now it hit him with the full force of a sledgehammer.

'You explain to me how come Bobby was graspin' that there gun in his right hand an' wearin' his holster tied down on his right thigh?' he rasped.

'Why in hell shouldn't he?' demanded Kane irritably, anxious now to be gone.

"Cause Bobby was left-handed, that's why!' retorted Ned Baines.

FOUR

When Ben Beardsley heard of Norton Kane's arrest for the murder of Bobby McCoy, he was naturally alarmed. Consequently, early on the morning after the murder, he paid Sheriff Luke Tanner a visit.

The law office consisted of a small front room, containing a desk, the sheriff's armchair, a couple of other chairs, a small pot-bellied stove and little else. This was where Tanner and his deputy spent much of their time. Here Tanner did his paperwork, brewed coffee, interviewed suspects and, for the greater part of the day, simply rested. The law office's rear quarters lay beyond this room, through a heavy oak door, which had a small barred window cut into it near the top. These comprised of no more than three cells and a narrow passage leading to a sturdy back door. It was in the middle cell that Norton Kane was lodged.

Beardsley noted with relief that the sheriff was alone. Johnnie Reid was evidently out patrolling the town. He slumped thankfully into the chair proffered him by Luke Tanner.

'Wa'al, what brings you here so bright 'n' early, Mr Mayor?' enquired the grizzled law-officer.

'I wanta know why yo're chargin' Norton Kane with murder?' said Beardsley.

'That's simple,' said Tanner. "Cause he gunned down an unarmed man, that's why.'

'I heard that Bobby McCoy was wearin' a gun.'

'Kane planted it on him after he shot him.'

Beardsley stared in some astonishment at the sheriff.

'How in tarnation d'you know that?' he demanded.

Slowly, patiently, Tanner explained, concluding sombrely, 'If Bobby had been right-handed like most folks, the murderin' bastard would have got away with it. Nobody could've proved it wasn't a fair fight.'

'Yeah. Wa'al, even so, nobody actually saw Kane gun him down an' then plant the Colt on him,' said Beardsley.

'Nope. But it's the only possible explanation.'

'I s'pose so, though I expect Kane denies it?'

"Course he does. He ain't got no wish to hang.'

'No.'

'That feller's a no-account critter, a real bad 'un, Ben.' Tanner shook his head sadly. 'I'm sorry you ever got mixed up with the sonofabitch. How'd you come to git tied in with him, anyways?'

'We was in the same huntin' party, is all,' lied the mayor. 'I ... I didn't hardly know the feller 'fore then.'

'But he saved yore life an' now you figure you owe him?'

'That's about it.'

'So, you've been bank-rollin' him ever since he hit town?'

'That's right, Luke.'

'Yet you knew he wasn't no good. Which is why you haven't exactly invited him into the bosom of yore family?'

'I had him over for Sunday lunch.'

'Once.'

'Yeah.' Beardsley sighed. 'Okay, I confess I don't like the man. I couldn't jest ignore him, though, not with him bein' kinda down on his luck. So, I guess I felt obliged to help him out. But I … I didn't expect him to stay in town this long. I reckoned on him moseyin' on out 'fore now.'

'Wa'al, he has sure overstayed his welcome,' said the sheriff.

'An' he looks likely to pay a pretty high price for doin' so.'

'Don't go feelin' sorry for him, Ben. If'n' I'm right, he shot down Bobby McCoy in cold blood. An' I don't s'pose Bobby's his first victim either.'

'Whaddya mean, Luke?'

'It's my belief Norton Kane is an outlaw, a man with a price on his head.'

'But he ain't wanted in the state of Kansas.'

'Not 'fore he gunned down Bobby; no.'

'So, why …?'

'I know the kind. I can almost smell 'em. An' then there's that business 'bout Boots Sutherland.'

'Who in tarnation is Boots Sutherland?'

'He was a bounty hunter.'

'Was?'

'Yup. He was ambushed an' killed ridin' through Cougar Pass.'

'When was that?'

'Seven weeks back. He was found lyin' there a coupla days after yore pal, Norton Kane, rode into Red Rock.'

'Who told you all this, Luke?'

'Pete Pearce. We meet up 'bout once a month to chew the fat an' discuss what's new in each other's territory.'

Ben Beardsley nodded. He knew of Luke Tanner's arrangement with Pete Pearce, the sheriff of the neighbouring town of Plainville.

'So what's this to do with Kane?' he asked.

'Wa'al, Pete an' me, we both agreed that Boots Sutherland had probably been on the trail of some desperado or other. An' we figured he got a mite careless, an' ended up bein' bushwhacked.'

'An' you believe the bushwhacker was Norton Kane?'

'Yup. Pete had earlier observed Sutherland ridin' through Plainville. An', as you know, the trail from Plainville winds its way through Couger Pass an' then leads directly to Red Rock.'

'The trail forks three ways when it leaves the pass,' commented Beardsley. 'One fork leads to Ellis, one to Victoria an' one to Red Rock. You cain't be sure which one was taken by Boots Sutherland's killer.'

'Nope. Nevertheless, Kane bein' in the vicinity, at the time the bounty hunter was killed, kinda points to his bein' the guilty party, wouldn't you say?'

'Mebbe.'

'Anyway, whatever past crimes he may or may not have committed an' got away with, I don't reckon Kane's gonna git away with this one.'

'Guess not. So, what have you done 'bout fixin' up a trial?'

'I've telegraphed Judge Jeremiah Hood, the circuit judge, an' also the Governor.'

'The Governor?'

'He'll need to send us one of his state prosecutors.'

'Of course.'

'An' Kane will need a defence attorney.'

'Yeah.' Beardsley grimaced. Lawyers never came cheap. 'I guess I'll have to hire one for him,' he muttered.

'Wa'al, Ben, Don't waste yore money on some big city dude. Whoever you employ, he won't git Kane off, not unless he can work miracles.'

Beardsley had a feeling that the sheriff was right. However, he also had a feeling that Norton Kane would insist upon being represented by the best defence attorney money could buy.

'May I go through an' have a few words with Kane?' he asked.

'Sure, help yoreself,' said Tanner.

The mayor was not looking forward to his interview with Norton Kane. But he dared not abandon the outlaw to his fate. He rose and went over and opened the heavy oak door. Then, he stepped into the narrow passage beyond and carefully closed the door behind him.

'Howdy, ole buddy. I was wonderin' when you'd show up,' said Kane, rising from his bunk in the middle one of the three cells.

Beardsley was relieved to note that the cells on either side of Kane's were both empty. He forced a weak smile.

'Howdy, Kane. A nice mess you've gotten yoreself into.'

Kane scowled.

'How was I to know the young lunkhead was left-handed?' he demanded angrily.

'But, why in tarnation did you kill him? Hell, he was only a boy!' exclaimed Beardsley.

'He humiliated me in front of the whole darned town. Nobody does that to Norton Kane an' lives.'

Beardsley stared hard at the gunslinger. The man wasn't just a common criminal. He was a goddam psychopath!

'You know anythin' 'bout the killin' of a certain Boots Sutherland?' enquired Beardsley.

Kane laughed harshly.

'Mebbe. Mebbe not,' he replied enigmatically.

'You know, Kane, you actually deserve to hang,' stated the mayor, his eyes filled with loathing.

'Do I, Ben? Wa'al, if 'n' I do hang, I might jest do a li'l singin' 'fore they put the rope round my neck.'

'Look, there's nuthin' much I can do to. ...'

'You could slip me a gun.'

'An' have you gun down the sheriff an' his deppity? Oh, no, Kane, I ain't gonna be no party to murder! Dammit, why didn't you try 'n' shoot yore way outa trouble when you was arrested?'

"Cause I wasn't expectin' to be arrested an' was kinda caught on the hop. 'Fore I could go for my gun, Tanner an' his pardner had me covered back 'n' front.'

'Yeah, wa'al, I ain't slippin' you no gun, but I'll tell you what I will do. I'll git you a lawyer,' said Beardsley.

As he had expected, Kane immediately rasped, 'I want the very best, Ben. A real hot-shot, not some hick from around these parts.'

'Understood, Kane,' replied Beardsley. 'I'll git you the best lawyer money can buy. There's a feller in Kansas city called Hiram Nettleton, they reckon is jest as smart as can be. If 'n' he cain't git you off, I guess nobody can.'

In fact, he doubted if anybody could save Norton Kane from the rope. But he refrained from saying as much. He had to hope that Hiram Nettleton could convince the jury of Kane's innocence, otherwise the gunman would hang. And, before he did.... It didn't bear thinking about. What would the revelation that he was an ex-bank robber, a man who had served seven years in Claxton County Jail, do to his wife and children? He felt murder in his heart. If he thought for one moment he could kill Kane and get away with it, he most assuredly would.

'When is my trial likely to take place, anyways?'

asked Kane.

'In about a week's time, mebbe less,' said Beardsley. 'Jest as soon as Judge Hood an' the state prosecutor can git here.'

'You'll have this Nettleton feller here by then, will you?'

'Providin' he's prepared to represent you.'

'But you ain't sure you can git him?'

'Nope, though I'm fairly confident. Lawyers don't as a rule turn down the offer of a big, fat fee.'

Kane grinned.

'Guess they don't at that,' he chuckled.

'So, it there's nuthin' else I can do for you...?' said Beardsley.

The outlaw interrupted him. He snapped his fingers, then made as though he was riffling through a roll of dollar bills. 'I could use a li'l cash,' he said.

'In here? Whaddya need cash for, in jail?'

'To buy a few luxuries. I ain't used to eatin' the swill the sheriff serves up to his prisoners.'

Beardsley scowled. He knew there was nothing wrong with the food that Luke Tanner provided. It was paid for out of municipal funds and was good, honest fare. Nonetheless, he counted out a generous wad of notes and handed them to the outlaw.

'That should take care of yore needs,' he said. 'An', now, reckon I'll be on my way, for I gotta attend church this mornin'.'

'Then, say a prayer for me, Ben. If I should want you for anythin', I'll ask the sheriff to let you know.'

'You do that.'

Ben Beardsley forced another smile and then beat a hasty retreat. He had no wish to pay Kane any further visits, yet he knew he would have to if summoned by the gunman.

Norton Kane, meanwhile, sank back onto his bunk and closed his eyes. Like the mayor, he had little hope that Hiram Nettleton could save him. For the lawyer to conduct a successful defence, he would require to be nothing less than a magician. Therefore, what Kane badly needed was a contingency plan, something to fall back upon should he be convicted.

He racked his brains, and, within a few minutes, it came to him. What he needed was some help to break out of jail. And the only people he could think of, who would be likely to come to his aid, were his old gang. They had split up in order to escape a pursuing posse of US marshals. The Grout brothers had made for Wichita, where they intended holing up with a cousin who owned a bordello. As for Travis Miller and Spence Delroy, they had headed for Dodge City. Miller's sister owned a dry goods store and some other real estate there and, consequently, Miller had anticipated finding cheap lodgings for the pair of them. Kane wished now that he had stuck with one or other party instead of riding off on his own. Certainly, he had shaken off the posse of US marshals, but then he had found the bounty-hunter, Boots Sutherland, hot on his trail. And it was the bounty-hunter who had forced him to ride down into Kansas and ultimately to Red Rock.

Kane cursed his luck. Then, when he had finished cursing, he began to consider how he might contact his old gang. It was as he mulled over this problem that he heard his name being whispered from outside his cell window.

'Mr Kane!'

He jumped up. A small barred window was cut into the rear wall of his cell. It was about head-high. Kane grabbed hold of the bars and peered out. A narrow alley ran behind the cells, between the law office and the stage line depot. This alley was rarely used and always lay in shadow. Kane grinned as he looked out and found himself staring into the foxy face of the Golden Garter's croupier, Rick Grainger.

'Howdy, Rick,' he said genially.

'Howdy, Mr Kane.' Grainger mopped his brow with a red silk handkerchief. He looked nervously up and down the alley, then reassured that nobody had spotted him, he enquired, 'You ... you okay, Mr Kane?'

'Are you tryin' to be funny?'

'Hell, no, Mr Kane! I ... I was jest naturally concerned an'. ...'

'Whaddya want, Rick?' demanded Kane. He had noticed the croupier's evident agitation and concluded that this was no ordinary social visit. 'Spit it out,' he said.

'Wa'al ... er ... I ... I jest wanted to ... to be sure you ain't gonna tell n-nobody that I supplied you with ... with that there g-gun, the one you ... er ... p-planted on B-Bobby McCoy,' stammered

Grainger.

Kane smiled through the bars at the croupier.

''Course not,' he said. 'I don't split on my pals.'

'No?'

'Nope. An' you are my pal, ain't you, Rick?'

'Sure am, Mr Kane.'

'Yo're the kinda pal that's always ready to do an ole buddy a favour.'

'What … what are you sayin', Mr Kane?'

'I'm saying' I want you to do me another small favour.'

'Oh, no!' Sweat beaded Grainger's brow and there was a look of horror in his eyes. 'No, Mr Kane, I ain't smugglin' you another gun. No, sirree!'

'I ain't said that I want you to git me another gun.'

'No, but yuh do, don't yuh? Yo're lookin' to shoot yore way outa jail.'

'An' if I am?'

'I ain't gittin' involved. Not this time. Goddammit, I didn't know you was plannin' to shoot Bobby McCoy, but I cain't claim that degree of ignorance on this occasion! You shoot the sheriff or his deppity with a gun I've supplied an' I'm sure as hell implicated!'

'Wa'al, like I said, I ain't asked you to git me another gun.' Kane paused. He would have liked Rick Grainger to smuggle him a gun, but he could see that the man was much too scared to do so. Grainger could, however, be useful in another way, for Kane had been wondering how he might get in touch with his old gang. He again smiled at the croupier and said softly, 'All I'm askin' you to do is send off a coupla telegraphs.'

The strained look slowly left Grainger's eyes and he nervously returned the outlaw's smile.

'Sure thing, Mr Kane. I'd be happy to do that for you. Who are you plannin' to telegraph?'

'Jest some ole buddies of mine.'

'I ... I guess, then, it'd be best if I rode over to Plainville an' sent them from the telegraph office over there,' said Grainger.

While he realised that telegraphs, like the US mail, were sacrosanct, nevertheless, he felt disinclined to have anyone in Red Rock, even the telegraph office clerk, know of his involvement with Kane.

'Jest as you like, Rick,' agreed the prisoner. 'Only you will send 'em off today, won't yuh?'

'Yeah. 'Course I will, Mr Kane.'

Kane did not absolutely trust the croupier, but he reckoned he could rely upon his greed.

'Here's twenty-five dollars for yore trouble,' he said, pushing part of the wad of notes Beardsley had given him through the bars.

'Gee, thanks, Mr Kane!' exclaimed Grainger, eagerly grabbing hold of the dollar bills.

'There's another twenty-five waitin' for you jest as soon as my ole buddies arrive in Red Rock. An', don't worry, you won't have to sneak along here to collect the money. I'll arrrange with one of the boys to hand it over to you.'

'On the quiet?'

'Of course.'

'So, what's the message an' who do you want it sendin' to?' asked Grainger, promptly producing a notebook and pencil from the inside pocket of his city-style jacket.

Kane thought for a moment. Then he began, 'The message is as follows: Am at Red Rock, Kansas. Need your help pronto. NK.'

'Brief an' to the point,' commented Grainger. 'An' to whom do I send this message?'

'You send one telegraph to Joe Grout, c/o The Pleasure Palace, Overland Street, Wichita, an' the other to Travis Miller, c/o Sarah's Store, Main Street, Dodge City.'

'Got it.'

'Good! Then, you'd best git goin', if yo're to ride to Plainville an' be back in time for yore evenin' stint at the Golden Garter.'

'Yeah, guess I had at that. Wa'al, I'll be seein' you, Mr Kane. S'long for now.'

'S'long Rick.'

Norton Kane watched the croupier scuttle off down the alleyway and disappear into Main Street. Since he was extremely doubtful whether Ben Beardsley's hot-shot lawyer would succeed in obtaining his acquittal, he was depending upon Grainger to keep his end of the bargain. Kane hoped that the prospect of receiving a further twenty-five dollars, when his gang rode into town, would persuade the croupier to fulfil his promise. If it did not, then Kane feared he would find himself dancing at the end of a rope before many days passed.

FIVE

Plainville was a dull town. That was indisputable. It had four saloons, but none was particularly lively. As Rick Grainger had told Norton Kane, none of them possessed a roulette wheel and nor did they have any ladies of easy virtue to entertain their customers.

Jack Stone was not particularly concerned about the former. Since it was his father's gambling which had lost the family farm back in Kentucky and so begun the chain of events that had conspired to make Stone an eternal rover, the Kentuckian had no desire whatsoever to play the wheel. He did, however, feel the need for a woman. For the last three months he had been on a cattle drive, riding the Western Trail from San Antonio, Texas, up to Julesberg, Nebraska. And now he had money to spend and was looking for some fun and relaxation. He had found little enough so far, but knew there would be entertainment in plenty to be had in Dodge City, which was where he was headed.

Six foot two inches tall and consisting of nigh on

two hundred pounds of muscle and bone, the Kentuckian was a pretty formidable character. He was remarkably quick for a big man and, although slow to anger, was as brave and dangerous as a mountain lion when roused. His square-cut, deeply lined face had been handsome once and now and again, when he smiled, it regained something of its former good looks.

He stood at the bar in the Red Light Saloon, smoking a cheroot and drinking whiskey. Around his strong, thick neck he had tied a red kerchief. A battered Stetson, threadbare grey shirt, faded denim pants over unspurred boots and a knee-length buckskin jacket completed the Kentuckian's wardrobe, while on his right thigh he wore a Frontier Model Colt tied down.

Stone had tried any number of perilous occupations in his time: cavalry scout, guard on the Overland stage, deputy US marshal, deputy sheriff and, most famously, sheriff of Mallory, where, as the man who tamed that hell-town, he had become a legend. But now all he wanted was to be left in peace, to work a little and play a little, and have no further need to use his gun. Unfortunately, though, Jack Stone was a man who attracted trouble as a magnet attracts metal.

The Kentuckian was onto his second whiskey when Rick Grainger came hurrying in through the batwing doors. The foxy-faced croupier had sent off the telegraphs as instructed by Norton Kane. He was relieved that he had done so, yet felt a touch guilty at the thought of what the outcome might be. Consequently, he had repaired forthwith to the Red Light Saloon, where he aimed to consume a large slug of red-eye.

As the croupier ordered the whiskey, Stone eyed him up and down. A glint of recognition brightened the Kentuckian's eye.

'Don't I know you from some place?' he growled.

The croupier started, then stepped back and gazed curiously at the gunfighter. Suddenly, he smiled.

'Holy cow! If it ain't Jack Stone!' he exclaimed.

'The same. But I cain't rightly put a name to yore face.'

'Rick Grainger.'

''Course! I remember now. You were a croupier at Sean O'Toole's Yellow Dog Saloon in Dodge City, same time as I was there as Bat Masterson's deppity.'

''Sright. Those were some times!'

'Sure were. Anyways, what're you doin' these days?'

'I'm still a croupier. Workin' over at Red Rock.'

Stone smiled.

'O'Toole dismiss you, did he?' he enquired.

'Why in tarnation would he do that? Why. ...'

'He'd do that 'cause you were skimmin' off some of the profits for yore own personal gain,' said Stone flatly.

Grainger opened his mouth to protest, but then thought better of it. He grinned sheepishly and shrugged his thin shoulders.

'Okay, so I admit it,' he said. 'Why not? It's

yesterday's news.'

'Red Rock must be a bit of a come-down after Dodge,' commented the Kentuckian.

'Aw, it ain't so bad.'

'Nope?'

'Nope. It sure beats this one-horse town. I tell you, Mr Stone, there's no place in Plainville to match the Golden Garter.'

'That where yo're workin'?'

'Sure is. We got what Plainville ain't got, an' that is a roulette wheel an' a parcel of pretty women jest itchin' to serve a man's every need.'

'Is that so?'

Stone grinned. Red Rock lay on the trail south to Dodge City. He had intended riding straight on through, but now he was tempted to stop over.

'Yessir,' said Grainger. 'I cain't hardly wait to git back.'

'So, if 'n' you don't care much for Plainville, what has brought you over here?' enquired Stone curiously.

'Oh ... er ... jest a li'l private business,' said Grainger evasively, and he hurried on, 'but that ... that's all taken care of, an' I intend leavin' town jest as soon as I've swallowed this here whiskey.'

'Mebbe I'll ride along with you,' said Stone.

'You headin' south, then?'

'Yup. As far as Dodge. I ain't long finished a cattle drive an' I got me some money to burn. Reckon mebbe I'll stop off an' spend a li'l of it at Red Rock. On one of them pretty women you spoke of.'

'Wa'al, you could do worse.' Grainger favoured Stone with a sidelong glance. 'You ain't wearin' no badge these days,' he observed.

'Nope. Like I said, I've been herdin' cattle.'

'So, you ain't been on the trail of Norton Kane?'

'Who's he?'

'I dunno exactly. Dresses all in black 'n' is mighty free with his money.'

'Some kinda dude, huh?'

'I don't think so. I figure he's a feller with a price on his head. That's why I wondered if you'd been on his trail.'

'Bounty-huntin' ain't my line. Never has been. But what's this feller doin' in Red Rock, anyways?'

'He was livin' it up pretty swell.'

'Was?'

'He's in jail for shootin' an unarmed cowpoke,' said Grainger, and he went on to explain the circumstances surrounding the violent death of Bobby McCoy, although omitting to mention his part in it.

When he had finished and had told the Kentuckian as much as he knew about the forthcoming trial, Stone scratched his jaw and drawled, 'Mebbe I'll stop over for more 'n' jest the one night. This here trial sounds as if it could be kinda interestin'.'

It could be a whole heap more interesting than Stone expected, thought Rick Grainger wryly, particularly if the jury returned a verdict of guilty and Norton Kane's old gang turned up and attempted to spring him. The croupier determined, therefore, to keep his wits about him on the day of the trial, for, if the bullets started flying, he had no wish to be anywhere near the line of fire. He finished his drink and slapped the empty glass down on the bar-counter.

'Wa'al, I'm gonna lam outa here,' he said. 'You comin', Mr Stone?'

'Yup.' Stone followed the other's example and tossed back the remains of his whiskey. 'I'm right with you,' he said.

Stone was taciturn by nature and Grainger had a great deal on his mind. The croupier was still half-afraid that Norton Kane might let slip the fact that he, Grainger, had supplied the gun which Kane had planted on Bobby McCoy. If he did, Grainger would have to leave Red Rock in a hurry. Not a prospect that appealed to him, for he enjoyed his job at the Golden Garter. Small-town it might be, yet it was safe and reasonably well paid. Consequently, neither man was inclined to converse much and the twenty miles between Plainville and Red Rock were completed mostly in silence.

Upon arrival in Red Rock, the two men parted, Rick Grainger to report for duty at the Golden Garter and Jack Stone to find a stable for his bay gelding and accommodation for himself. The former he found in Ben Beardsley's livery stables and the latter in Ma French's rooming-house. Then, when he had freshened up a little, the Kentuckian made his way along Main Street to Flanagan's Saloon.

A number of the town's hierarchy clustered round the bar. All except Doc Brady and Sheriff Luke Tanner were members of Red Rock's town council. They comprised of Harry Lewin the owner of the Grand Hotel, Garfield Tills who managed the town's only bank, Felix Oates the mortician, four of the town's storekeepers and Red Rock's most prominent citizen, its mayor. They were discussing the forthcoming trial, though Ben Beardsley uncharacteristically had little to say on the subject. He was struggling hard to maintain a bold front, but in truth he was a very worried man.

Stone ordered a beer and leant against the bar. He had a fearful thirst on him and he emptied the glass in one draught. The second beer took him rather longer to consume and, as he stood at the bar drinking, the Kentuckian could not help but overhear the others' conversation.

All of them seemed to think Norton Kane would be found guilty of the murder of Bobby McCoy and would hang, though, knowing of their mayor's connection with the accused, they were careful not to be too damning in their judgment. For his sake, they talked of the possibility of extenuating circumstances. None, however, really believed that these existed.

The next man through the batwing doors was not so considerate of Ben Beardsley's feelings.

Jim Pelham was a big man with a craggy, weatherbeaten face and faded blue eyes. He wore a smart white Stetson, an expensive cotton shirt, a neat boot-lace tie, knee-length black coat, tailor-made trousers and gleaming black leather riding-boots. All in all, the rancher cut a pretty impressive figure. He pushed his way through the batwing doors and strode purposefully across the bar-room to where Red Rock's hierarchy were holding forth. Marching up to Ben Beardsley, he stabbed a finger in the mayor's face and shouted belligerently, 'Yo're responsible for this, you sonofabitch! If you hadn't invited that no-account critter Kane into Red Rock. ...'

'I didn't invite him here,' retorted Beardsley.

'Wa'al, he's yore pal.'

'Nope. He ain't no pal of mine. He saved my life 'bout ten years back. So, I reckon I owe him. That don't mean we're buddies, though.'

'Hmm. Wa'al. ...'

'An', like I said, I didn't invite him to Red Rock. He was jest passin' through when he chanced to recognise me.'

'That's true. I'll vouch for that,' said Frank Flanagan from behind the bar.

'So, mebbe you didn't invite him here, but you sure as hell encouraged him to stay,' snapped Pelham. 'It's common knowledge you've been bank-rollin' Kane ever since he got to Red Rock.'

Beardsley frowned. Nobody knew that for certain. They were simply guessing. But what was the point of denying it? He shrugged his shoulders.

'Yes,' he said. 'I've been bank-rollin' him. Kane was down on his luck an' I reckoned I couldn't do no other than give him a few bucks to tide him over.'

'Which is why he stayed on.'

'I s'pose.'

'So, it's yore goddam fault he was around to kill young Bobby!' cried Pelham.

'If you like to look at it that way, I guess it is,' said Beardsley. 'But put yoreself in my place, Jim. What would you have done?'

'I ain't in yore place, Ben,' rasped Pelham. 'An' I ain't arguin' with you. I'm holdin' you responsible. So, what're you gonna do 'bout it?'

'Nuthin' I can do. Kane's in jail awaitin' trial. You'll need to let justice take its course.'

'I could ride in here with my boys an' take the town apart,' said Pelham.

'I wouldn't advise it,' interjected Sheriff Luke Tanner.

'No?'

'Nope. I know Bobby was one of yore men an'. ...'

'He was almost like a son to me.'

Luke Tanner nodded sympathetically. Bobby McCoy had been a cheerful, happy-go-lucky eighteen year old, easy to get on with and, by all accounts, darned good at his work. He hadn't an enemy in the world and would be missed by more than just the hands on the Bar Q ranch.

'Yeah. Wa'al, I can 'preciate yore anger, Mr Pelham, but takin' the law into yore own hands won't solve nuthin',' said the sheriff.

Jim Pelham glared at the lawman.

'If it wasn't for yore goddam law forbiddin' the boys from carryin' firearms into town on Saturday nights, Bobby wouldn't've been unarmed when Kane gunned him down,' snarled the rancher.

'That ordinance has worked pretty well over the years,' said Harry Lewin. 'You know it has, Jim. Hell, you an' Les Gates was only sayin' as much a coupla weeks back!'

Jim Pelham frowned. This was true. He and Les Gates had been congratulating themselves on the fact that, since Luke Tanner's ordinance had been enforced, there had been no serious incident between the hands of the Bar Q and Lazy S ranches. An occasional fist-fight, but nothing more. As ranch-owners they had had every reason to be pleased with the ban on firearms. Until now, that is.

'Wa'al, I dunno. ...'

''Course it has,' said Garfield Tills.

The other council members added their voices to this argument, and Jim Pelham eventually capitulated.

'Okay! Okay!' he said. 'So, when's this here trial due to be held?'

'Judge Jeremiah Hood is already on his way. He's expected to ride into town sometime on Thursday,' said Tanner.

'I guess, then, that the trial will take place on Friday?'

'That's right.'

'I'll be there. That's for sure.'

'Come alone. Don't bring none of your boys. We

don't want no trouble,' said Tanner.

The rancher nodded. He was still very angry, but he was nobody's fool, and he realised that it would be best if his men remained on the ranch during the course of the trial. In their present mood, they were quite capable of lynching Kane, which would be rather stupid when the sonofabitch was likely to hang anyway.

'Okay,' he grunted. 'I'll mebbe bring Ned Baines an' a coupla the older hands. But the rest of the boys I'll leave behind. You got my word on that.'

So saying, he turned to go.

'Won't you stay 'n' have a drink with us?' enquired Garfield Tills genially.

The rancher shook his head.

'I ain't drinkin' in this town till the folks here have delivered their verdict an' Norton Kane is dancin' at the end of a rope,' he stated flatly, and, with that, he stormed off out of the saloon.

'Whew!' sighed Luke Tanner, as the batwing doors swung to behind him. The sheriff mopped his brow.

'Ole Jim was pretty steamed up!' commented Doc Brady.

'I don't blame him,' said Harry Lewin.

'Nor do I. But, I tell you, I'll be glad when this darned trial is over an' we can git back to normal,' said Tanner.

'Me too,' said Harry Lewin, though, in fact, he was secretly hoping the trial would bring him in some extra hotel business.

Felix Oates the mortician had a similar

thought. He was happily anticipating taking Norton Kane's measurements.

Following the departure of Jim Pelham, they all felt in need of another drink. Ben Beardsley gave the necessary order and Frank Flanagan set to work to fill it.

Jack Stone, meantime, had finished his second beer. He placed the empty glass on the counter. What he wanted now was a nice, juicy steak and, afterwards, a nice, juicy woman.

SIX

In the days that followed, Red Rock was roused out of its usual torpor. Apart from on Saturday nights, when the cowboys rode into town, there was little or no excitement in the small prairie town. For the next few days, however, that was all changed.

First of all, the lawyers arrived on the noonday stage. Both were city clad, wearing expensive three-piece suits and derby hats. But there the similarity ended. Hiram Nettleton, the attorney engaged to defend Norton Kane, was short, fat, middle-aged and totally bald, with his eyes owl-like behind their spectacles. The state prosecutor, on the other hand, was a tall, lean, lank-haired young man of no more than twenty-three summers. He possessed a thin, sallow face, an aquiline nose and piercing black eyes beneath beetling black eyebrows. Nettleton looked as though he had already made a reputation for himself, while Steve Morris clearly still had his to make.

The two lawyers had adjoining rooms at the

Grand Hotel and, as strangers in town, they tended to seek each other's company, dining together and afterwards relaxing over a few drinks in Flanagan's Saloon. This did not mean that each would not do his utmost to demolish the other's case in court. On the contrary, once the trial began, the two advocates would stop at nothing in order to win. To this end, both spent the best part of each day studying the case. Both interviewed the sheriff and his deputy and, while Hiram Nettleton spent long hours closeted with his client, Steve Morris carefully interrogated all those who had arrived upon the scene of the shooting. He was particularly interested in what Ned Baines and the other cowpokes from the Bar Q had to say, for it was upon their evidence that the case for the prosecution was founded.

Jack Stone observed the lawyers hurrying hither and thither, and he watched as various folk from in and around the county descended upon Red Rock, anxious to see the trial. Most arrived on the Thursday, some from the neighbouring towns of Plainville and Ellis, but mainly homesteaders from within a short radius of Red Rock. A couple of reporters from Dodge City and Abilene booked in at the Grand Hotel, while most of the others who needed overnight accommodation chose cheaper lodgings such as Ma French's rooming-house. The remainder prepared to while away the night in either Flanagan's or the Golden Garter.

Judge Jeremiah Hood rode into town just as dusk was beginning to fall. A tall, severe-looking individual, in a black frock-coat and black trousers, and sporting a slightly battered black stove-pipe hat, the judge sat astride a splendid black stallion. He dismounted in front of the Court House, where he was promptly met by the sheriff and Ben Beardsley and his fellow-councillors, all of whom had been closeted inside, awaiting his arrival.

Arrangements for the trial were discussed and finalised. Then Ben Beardsley escorted Judge Hood to his home, where his wife Jessica had prepared a meal and a room for Red Rock's distinguished visitor.

The judge's arrival was also observed by Jack Stone. The Kentuckian had appropriated one of the rockers which stood on the stoop outside Flanagan's Saloon, and here he spent much of his time, smoking cheroots, drinking beer, quietly watching the various comings and goings and generally relaxing. He nodded amiably to the deputy, young Johnnie Reid, as the youth commenced his evening rounds of the town.

'Tomorrow's the day, then?' he said.

'Yup. Tomorrow's the day,' said Johnnie Reid cheerfully.

The young deputy was tickled pink to have met the man who had tamed Mallory, the gunfighter who had stood side by side with the great Bat Masterson. It was not every day he encountered someone really famous. Luke Tanner, on the other hand, was rather less impressed, although he, too, was happy enough to have the Kentuckian in town. He had boasted how peaceful a community Red Rock was, and Stone, in consequence, reckoned on a reasonably quiet stay.

Ten minutes after Judge Hood had disappeared into Ben Beardsley's fine two-storey, red brick house, the Kentuckian changed his mind on that score. He immediately recognised the two men who rode into town through the gathering darkness and reined in their horses before Flanagan's Saloon. What was more to the point, they both recognised him.

A few years back Travis Miller and Spence Delroy had attempted to hold up a stagecoach on which Stone was riding shotgun. They had failed miserably. Although they had escaped, they had not escaped unscathed. Miller had a stiff left leg to this day, while Spence Delroy was minus his left ear.

Travis Miller was the taller of the two, a lean man with a sharp, bony, pockmarked face and a mouthful of blackened teeth. He was unshaven and his blond, sunbleached hair hung down to his shoulders. His Stetson had once been white. It was now a grubby grey and badly travel-stained. He wore a faded blue shirt, a black leather vest and faded denims. His boots were scuffed and he had the air of a man who had known better times. His horse, though, was a sturdy bay gelding and Stone noted grimly that he wore a Remington in his holster and carried a Winchester in his saddleboot.

Spence Delroy was of about medium height, of a

solid, squat build and heavily bearded. His clothes
were just as travel-soiled as his pardner's, but,
where Miller wore a vest over his shirt, Delroy
sported a hip-length brown leather jerkin. He
rode a grey mare and was similarly armed,
although, in addition to the firearms, he carried a
Bowie knife in a sheath at his waist.

'Wa'al, if it ain't that celebrated lawman, Jack
Stone!' sneered Travis Miller.

'Howdy, boys,' said Stone evenly.

The Kentuckian seemed quite at his ease,
rocking gently back and forwards in the rocker. In
fact, he was as tense as a coiled spring, his jacket
flipped open so that he could reach and draw his
Frontier Model Colt without impediment.

'Is this jest a coincidence, you bein' here in Red
Rock, or are you mebbe lookin' for us?' demanded
Delroy suspiciously.

'Bounty-huntin' ain't Stone's line; is it, Stone?'
said Miller.

'Nope.'

'An', since we ain't wanted in this here state, I
don't reckon you got any quarrel with us? Huh?'

'Nope.'

'So, is there another saloon in town?'

'Right on down the street.'

'Thanks.'

Stone watched with hooded eyes as the two
gunslingers urged their horses forward and rode
on down Main Street in the direction of the
Golden Garter. He had expected to face a
showdown and he was both surprised and relieved

that they had thought better of it. The icy lump, which Stone always felt in the pit of his stomach when his life was on the line, began to melt. Even so, he was puzzled. Travis Miller and Spence Delroy were mean, cold-blooded killers. They were many things, most of which were pretty bad, but they were not cowards. And they had reason to hate Stone. If someone had given him a game leg or shot off his ear, he wouldn't be likely to forego the chance of revenge. Yet they had ignored the opportunity of a shoot-out and had simply ridden on. Why?

The Kentuckian knew little about the two outlaws, other than the fact that they operated as a pair. What, he wondered, had brought them to Red Rock? A rendezvous, perhaps? If so, with whom and for what purpose? Stone determined to keep an eye on them. He would let them settle in at the Golden Garter and then, later, he would look in to see what they were up to. In the meantime, the Kentuckian intended to finish his beer and his cheroot and then go find the sheriff. It would be as well if Luke Tanner knew of the presence in Red Rock of the two desperadoes.

While Jack Stone continued to rock backwards and forwards on the stoop outside Flanagan's Saloon, Travis Miller and Spence Delroy trotted slowly through the town towards Red Rock's one and only rival establishment.

'We should've taken Stone,' snarled Delroy angrily.

'No, we shouldn't,' snapped Miller. 'We're here

to help Norton. That's our reason for bein' in Red Rock.'

'So?'

'So, we don't do nuthin' to draw attention to ourselves. We can take Stone later, but first we gotta find Norton an' discover jest why he needs our help.'

'An' how do we do that, Travis?'

'We find ourselves a drunk an' git him into conversation. There ain't nobody like the town soak to let you know what's happenin' in town.'

As Miller spoke, they found themselves in front of the Golden Garter. They reined in their horses, dismounted and tethered the two animals to the rail at the foot of the steps leading up to the stoop. Then they clattered up the steps, crossed the stoop and entered the saloon through the batwing doors.

The forthcoming trial had done Dan Evans' establishment no harm whatsoever. It was jam-packed. All the tables were taken. Blackjack and poker were much in demand, while the crowd was three deep round the roulette wheel. The bar-counter, too, was thronged with drinkers and the saloon-girls were doing brisk business. Dan Evans stood at one end of the bar-counter, smoking a large cigar and looking very pleasd with himself.

Miller and Delroy made their way to the opposite end and ordered whiskies. They did not, however, have to engage the local drunk in conversation. The talk all around them was

confined to one subject only: the trial of Norton
Kane for the murder of Bobby McCoy. They had
not been in the Golden Garter for more than ten
minutes before they knew all they needed to
know, including the fact that Kane was incarcer-
ated in one of the cells at the rear of the law office.

The two outlaws moved away from the bar,
crossed the saloon floor and, pushing open the
batwing doors, stepped out onto the stoop. They
stood there for a few moments, silently sipping
their whiskies. Then Spence Delroy spoke in a low
voice.

'So, that's why Norton sent for us,' he said. 'He
wants us to spring him.'

'Wa'al, whaddya reckon?' said Miller.

'I reckon I'd best mosey on over an' take a look
at the law office. Kinda size up the job.'

'Yeah.'

'You wait here, Travis; I'll be back in a few
minutes.'

Delroy drained the remains of his whiskey and
handed the empty glass to his confederate. Then
he made his way across Main Street to the
opposite sidewalk. He sauntered slowly up it in
the direction of Flanagan's Saloon. Passing the
law office, he glanced inside, noting the small,
sparsely-furnished front room. Johnnie Reid was
out on his rounds, so only the elderly sheriff
remained inside. He was busily making himself a
fresh pot of coffee. Spence Delroy smiled thinly.
He reckoned he and Miller could easily take the
sheriff if need be.

The dark alleyway between the law office and the stage line depot was like an open invitation to the gunman. Delroy slipped into it without a second thought. He eased his way along it until he reached the first of the barred windows looking into the cells. He peered in through the bars. The cell was dark and empty. The second was also dark, but he could hear the sound of some heavy breathing.

'Norton?' he whispered urgently.

'Yup. Who's that?'

'Spence Delroy.'

Norton Kane's thin features promptly appeared out of the gloom, on the opposite side of the bars.

'Howdy, Spence.'

'You've gotten yoreself into a fine ole mess.'

'Sure have. That's why I sent for you an' Travis. Where is Travis, by the way?'

'At the Golden Garter. You want us to spring you?'

'If'n I'm found guilty.'

'You reckon you can beat the rap?'

'Mebbe. I got me a hot-shot lawyer.'

'Hmm. It might be easier to spring you 'fore the trial takes place. Me 'n' Travis could take out that ole sheriff an'. ...'

'Don't underestimate Tanner. He's mebbe past his prime, but he ain't no push-over. 'Sides he's gonna have company. He an' his deppity are both aimin' to remain on guard here, right up until I'm taken into court at nine tomorrow mornin'.'

'He's on his own at the moment.'

'Deppity's doin' the rounds, I guess. But he'll be back.'

'There'll be other rounds to make. Later on. We can wait until one or other leaves the office an' then. ...'

'Both of 'em are pretty keyed up, I can tell you. So, it won't be easy to take whoever's left by surprise. No, sirree! There's bound to be shootin' an' that's gonna alert folks. They'll come pourin' outa the Golden Garter 'fore you can say Jack. Releasin' me from this here cell an' gittin' clear of the law office 'fore they bust in could prove a mite tricky.'

Spence Delroy considered this, and he had to admit that Kane had a point.

'Okay. So, what's yore plan?' he asked.

'It's simple. If I'm found guilty tomorrow, the sheriff an' his deppity will have to bring me back here to wait till a gallows has been erected.'

'That could take a coupla days or more.'

'Wa'al, I ain't plannin' on waitin' that long. No, I want you an' the boys. ...'

'The boys?'

'I also sent for the Grout brothers.'

Delroy nodded. All the old gang together again.

'We was once a darned good outfit,' he said.

'Sure was.'

Norton Kane smiled in the darkness. None of them had done anywhere near as well either before or since the time they had ridden together. And he had been their leader. It had always been his plans that they had followed. Eventually,

though, they had been forced to split up to escape
the law. But now, perhaps, it was time to reunite.
Kane was banking on the others to be thinking
the same. If they wanted to badly enough, they
would take a gamble and spring him from jail. If
they didn't. ...

'You was gonna tell me your plan,' Delroy
interrupted his train of thought.

'Yeah. Wa'al, what I figure is this: you an' Travis
attend the trial while the Grout brothers, they wait
up the street at Flanagan's Saloon. Then, when the
jury retire to reach their verdict, Travis leaves the
Court House an' hightails it to Flanagan's to alert
the brothers. Whereupon, they head for this here
law office an' break in through the rear door. That's
supposing it's locked, which it may not be. You,
meantime, wait in the Court House for the jury to
deliver their verdict. Okay, so far?'

'Okay.'

'Good! Then, you, in turn, head for the rear of
the law office. There's an alleyway between it an'
the Court House which you can cut down. You tell
the others whether or not I've been found guilty. If
I've been acquitted, you can all simply skedaddle,
an' we'll meet up at Flanagan's.'

'An' if'n yo're found guilty?'

'The sheriff an' his deppity are dead certain to
bring me back here through the rear doors of both
the Court House an' the law office. So, all you
gotta do is lie in wait for 'em, take 'em by surprise
an' lay 'em out. Then, you free me an' we all slip
out the back, where we wait while a couple of you

goes 'n' fetches yore horses, not forgettin' to bring a spare mount for me.'

'Hmm. Sounds pretty neat.'

'It is. We'll be half-way to Nebraska 'fore anyone knows I've been sprung.'

'Yeah. Could be at that.'

'Then, you'll do it?'

'Providin' the Grout brothers turn up.'

Norton Kane nodded. There was strength in numbers.

'They'll be here,' he said confidently.

'I hope so.' A thought suddenly struck Spence Delroy. 'By the way, Norton,' he said, 'how d'you manage to telegraph me 'n' Travis? You couldn't hardly ask the sheriff to send that there message.'

Kane laughed softly.

'Nope. I got Rick Grainger, the croupier at the Golden Garter, to send off telegraphs both to you an' Travis an' to the Grout brothers. I paid him twenty-five dollars for his trouble, with the promise of another twenty-five if 'n when you all hit town.'

'That ain't much.'

'It was enough. The feller's a cheap-jack.'

'So, how're you gonna pay him the second twenty-five?'

'I ain't. I told him I'd arrange for one of you boys to pay him.'

'It'll need to be done kinda discreetly.'

'It won't need to be done at all.'

'Whaddya mean?'

'I mean, Spence, that I don't want Rick

Grainger to know you've arrived in Red Rock.'

'You reckon he'd blab?'

'He might. Fifty dollars ain't nowhere near enough to buy someone like Grainger's loyalty.'

'If'n he did blab, he'd incriminate hisself.'

'Mebbe. Depends. Anyways, jest in case he gits any qualms of conscience, I figure it'd be best if he was silenced. Permanently.'

Spence Delroy's eyes glittered malevolently. The prospect of killing someone always excited him. He had the killer instincts of a wolverine and derived a sadistic, almost sensual pleasure, from the act of murder.

'I'll take care of the feller ... personally,' he promised.

'Thanks, Spence. I knew I could rely on you to oblige me.'

'Yeah. Wa'al, guess I'd best git back to the Golden Garter. Mebbe the Grout boys will have hit town by now?'

'Mebbe? Anyways, see you tomorrow after the trial.'

'Yup. Be seein' you, Norton.'

Spence Delroy left an optimistic Norton Kane to spend what he hoped would be one last night in his cell. The appearance of Delroy at the barred window had cheered him immensely.

Delroy, for his part, returned to the Golden Garter to find that, in his absence, the Grout brothers had indeed arrived in Red Rock. They had reined up in front of the saloon and spied Travis Miller standing outside on the stoop,

clutching a couple of empty whiskey glasses and
puffing nervously on a cheroot. He had explained
what he and Delroy had found out and had told
the Grout brothers the conclusions they had
drawn. Then, he and the brothers had adjourned
to the bar, where Delroy eventually found them.

There were three brothers, burly, thickset
fellows similarly attired in travel-stained Stet-
sons, check shirts, black leather vests and levis.
Each of them carried a Remington revolver in his
holster and a Winchester rifle in his saddleboot,
and each looked as though he was accustomed to
using both weapons.

Joe Grout was the oldest of the trio, and it
showed. His hair was liberally speckled with grey,
as was his short, square-cut beard. At some stage
in his violent career, he had evidently lost his left
eye, for he wore a black patch over the now-empty
socket.

The other two, while they did not sport
fully-grown beards, looked as though they had not
shaved for two or three days. Tom, the elder of the
two, bore a livid white scar on his right cheek, the
relic of a knife-fight, while young Sam was
surprisingly unmarked.

All three were anxious to hear Spence Delroy's
news, as was Travis Miller.

'Wa'al,' growled Miller, 'were we right in our
assumption?'

Delroy nodded. He glanced about him. The
crowd had thinned a little at their end of the bar.
Therefore, he gestured to the others to close in on

him and then, in a few succinct, well-chosen
words, he whispered Kane's plan to them. When
he had finished, there was a short silence. Since
nobody seemed keen to break it, Delroy continued
quietly, 'Me 'n' Travis, we figure on participatin' in
this li'l scheme; don't we, Travis?'

'Guess so,' said Miller.

'What about you boys?' asked Delroy.

'We ain't come all this way jest to sit back an' do
nuthin',' said Joe Grout.

'So, yo're in, all three of you?'

Joe Grout looked at his younger brothers. They
both nodded enthusiastically.

'Yup,' he said.

'Good! Wa'al, there's jest one other thing needs
attendin' to,' said Delroy, and he went on to explain
how Norton Kane wanted Rick Grainger taken
care of.

Much to the others' relief, he volunteered to take
on this job, which he proposed to do later, when the
saloon closed. For the present, he suggested, 'Since
there ain't nuthin' much else we can do tonight,
let's jest relax an' enjoy ourselves. An', as I guess
we ain't about to stick together for the whole of the
night, I suggest we fix some place to meet
tomorrow.'

'Suits me,' said Joe Grout.

'Where d'you suggest?' asked his brother, Tom.

'I observed a small eatin'-house up the street,
next door to the barberin' parlour. We'll meet there
tomorrow at eight o'clock sharp for breakfast,' said
Delroy. 'For now, though, I'm gonna have me a few

more drinks an' then I reckon I'll see if'n I can find myself a woman,' he added, with a chuckle.

'That sounds good,' said Travis Miller.

The others nodded their agreement and another round of whiskies was promptly ordered.

For the next couple of hours or so, all five remained drinking at the bar and talking over old times. Then, one by one, they drifted away. The two younger Grouts disappeared upstairs with a couple of Dan Evans' young ladies, while Joe Grout went across and sat in on a game of poker. Travis Miller, for his part, had earlier had an eyeful of Kitty's voluptuous charms and, therefore, he waited until she was available and then sidled over and engaged her in conversation. A few minutes later, he and she made their way upstairs, Miller clutching a bottle of the Golden Garter's 'champagne' in one hand and eagerly pinching Kitty's bottom with the other.

This left Spence Delroy drinking alone at the bar. He finished his whiskey and sauntered across the saloon towards the roulette wheel, where Rick Grainger was being kept pretty busy. Dan Evans was also in close attendance, viewing the substantial takings with a proprietorial eye. The outlaw promptly buttonholed him.

'How long d'you reckon to keep open tonight?' enquired Delroy.

'Till we run outa customers,' replied the saloon-keeper jovially.

'An' when's that likely to be?'

'On a good night like tonight, not much 'fore

four in the mornin', I guess. Why d'you ask?'

'Wa'al, I figured on playin' the wheel, but first I was lookin' to amuse myself with one of yore gals.'

'You got time for both.'

'Yeah, s'pose I have at that.'

Delroy smiled at the saloon-keeper and strolled off, back towards the bar. There was a little redhead there who had the looks of an angel, but who, considering her profession, had to know a thing or two. He would take her to bed and then later, when there were no witnesses, he would deal with Rick Grainger. He could scarcely contain his delight. He was really going to enjoy tonight. Fornication and murder were, after all, his two favourite pastimes.

The outlaw would not have felt quite so delighted, however, had he realised that his and Travis Miller's rendezvous with the Grout brothers had been observed by Jack Stone.

The Kentuckian had warned Sheriff Luke Tanner of the presence in Red Rock of the two known desperadoes, and the sheriff had been duly concerned. Since he and Johnnie Reid were likely to have their hands full for the next twenty-four hours with the forthcoming trial, Tanner had gladly accepted Stone's offer to keep a close eye on the outlaws. Consequently, Stone had made his way across to the Golden Garter and, from the opposite end of the bar, maintained a discreet watch on the five gunslingers.

Now, as Spence Delroy vanished upstairs with the redhead, Stone decided it was time to retire to

Ma French's rooming-house. Four of his suspects were closeted with Dan Evans' girls, while the fifth was deeply involved in what seemed likely to be an all-night game of poker. He reckoned, therefore, that he could safely retire and resume his surveillance in the morning.

The Kentuckian had no idea as to the identity of the Grout brothers, but his instincts told him that they were bad news. The five men together spelt big trouble. Of that he was convinced. Usually these days, Stone avoided trouble like the plague, yet here he was volunteering to involve himself in what could easily turn out to be a pretty explosive situation. What in tarnation had made him do it, he asked himself? A conscience that would not let him stand idly by while evil was perpetrated? A desire to scupper Delroy and Miller's little game, whatever it might be? He didn't really know. He smiled wryly and downed the remains of his whiskey. Then he left the saloon and walked slowly and thoughtfully back to his rooming-house.

SEVEN

It was three o'clock in the morning when Spence Delroy left the redhead. She was somewhat surprised at his abrupt departure and cajoled him to remain with her.

'I ain't likely to git me no more customers tonight,' she murmured. 'So, why don't you stay?'

Delroy was tempted, but he shook his head and continued dressing.

''Nother time,' he drawled.

The redhead pouted, shrugged her pretty shoulders and, turning her back on him, snuggled down again and pulled the blankets up over her head. Delroy grinned and strapped on his gun-belt. Then he pulled on his Stetson and quietly left the room.

Downstairs, he found the bar-room almost deserted. Only one poker game continued, that in which Joe Grout was participating, and there were few gamblers left at the roulette wheel. Delroy grabbed an empty chair at the roulette table and, for the next hour, tried his luck with the wheel. He did pretty well and was over one hundred dollars in profit when, eventually, he found himself to be the last remaining player. The poker game, he observed, was also breaking up.

'You wantin' to continue?' enquired the croupier.

'Nope. Guess I'll quit while I'm still ahead,' said Delroy.

'Holy cow! A gamblin' man with some good ole hoss sense!' Rick Grainger grinned, then yawned and confessed, 'I'm whacked. Cain't hardly wait to hit the sack.'

'Wa'al, you'll need to wait a while yet,' said Delroy, whereupon he lowered his voice to a whisper and said, 'Norton Kane wants to see you. Now.'

Rick Grainger eyed the stranger with unconcealed alarm.

'You … you one of them fellers Kane telegraphed?' he murmured.

'Yup.'

'Hell!' The croupier had been half-hoping that Norton Kane's gang would fail to respond to the telegraphs he had sent. Being an extremely avaricious man, he naturally wanted the second payment of twenty-five dollars promised by the accused, yet, at the same time, he feared the consequences of his sending those two telegraphs. Were the rest of the gang here, he wondered nervously? 'Kane said one of you would pay me twenty-five dollars, that I needn't trouble to collect it off him,' he muttered.

'Mebbe he changed his mind?'

'But. ...'

'Wa'al, it's up to you. If'n you want the money, you'll do as he asks,' said Delroy.

'I guess so.' Grainger looked rather unhappy at the prospect.

'Where d'you live, by the way?' asked Delroy.

'I gotta room upstairs at the back of the saloon.'

'Is there a rear exit?'

'Yeah. There's a flight of steps at the back.'

'Then, if I was you, I'd go that way. Less chance of anyone spottin' you.'

Rick Grainger nodded. He glanced anxiously across the saloon towards the bar, where Dan Evans was chatting to the two bartenders. The saloon-keeper was in high good humour and only waiting for the poker players to depart before locking up his establishment. Grainger forced himself to shout a cheery good-night and then hurried off upstairs.

Spence Delroy, meantime, was joined by Joe Grout, who, unlike his confederate, had not been favoured by Lady Luck. He was not, therefore, in the sunniest of moods.

'Wa'al?' he grunted grumpily.

'It's all set up,' said Delroy, with a wicked grin. 'All you gotta do is bring a coupla hosses round back of the saloon. I'll take care of our croupier friend.'

'Are you sure about this? Cain't we jest pay the feller his twenty-five dollars an' ...?'

'Norton said to silence him. Permanently,' snarled Delroy.

Joe Grout studied the other's face. The heavy beard and the missing ear gave Spence Delroy an almost piratical appearance. But it was the eyes which were truly frightening. They were like black pits, chilling and fathomless and utterly devoid of any pity, the eyes of a pathological killer. Joe Grout had himself killed many men in his time, but it had always been in the heat of the moment. He could not do what Delroy proposed, gun down an unarmed man in cold blood. He shrugged his shoulders.

'I'll git the hosses,' he said, as they pushed their way through the batwing doors and stepped outside onto the stoop.

Spence Delroy nodded and, dropping down from the sidewalk, he turned and made his way silently along the side of the saloon. At its rear, just as Rick Grainger had described, there was a flight of wooden steps leading to the upper storey. Delroy crouched in the shadows at the bottom of these steps and waited.

He did not have long to wait. Above him a door quietly opened and closed. Then, he heard the sound of furtive footsteps descending. Slowly, Delroy withdrew the Remington from his holster. He reversed the gun and, holding it by the barrel, raised it above his head. He watched the croupier cautiously step down onto the ground and peer back up at the door through which he had just made his exit. Smiling sadistically, Delroy sprang forward and brought the butt of the revolver crashing down on Rick Grainger's unsuspecting skull.

The croupier went down as though poleaxed. He hit the dust with a dull thud and lay quite still. Delroy was crouched down examining him when Joe Grout appeared with the two horses.

'You … you killed him already?' gasped Grout.

'Nope. Jest KO'd him. Here, help me sling him over the saddle of yore horse.'

Between them, the two gunslingers had little trouble draping Rick Grainger's small, lean frame over the saddle of Joe Grout's chestnut gelding. They secured him firmly with some cord and then Delroy mounted his grey mare and, with his left hand, took hold of the gelding's reins.

'I'll see you an' the others at about eight o'clock, at that eatin'-house we spoke of,' he drawled.

'What are you plannin' to do with him?' asked Grout, glancing at the inert form of the croupier.

'I'm gonna kill him, of course.'

'So, where are you takin' him?'

'As far away from Red Rock as I can git. We sure as hell don't want nobody to discover his cadaver. Leastways, not till we're long gone.'

'That's true.' Joe Grout smiled thinly. 'Be seein' you, then, Spence,' he said.

'Yup.'

Spence Delroy was as good as his word. He had four hours to ride out and back, if he was to rendezvous with the others at eight o'clock as planned. Therefore, he proposed to head due south for approximately two hours, and then stop and finish off his victim and hide the corpse.

For the best part of those two hours, Rick

Grainger remained unconscious. Then, slowly, gradually, he regained his senses. In consequence, for the last fifteen to twenty minutes, Delroy was forced to listen to the croupier pleading for his life. Grainger's whining and snivelling did nothing, however, to persuade Delroy to exercise clemency.

The outlaw reined in the two horses on the edge of a stand of cottonwoods. He climbed out of the saddle and went over and released Grainger from his bonds. The foxy-faced croupier slipped off the gelding's saddle and fell in a heap on the ground, where he tried to rub some life into his numbed limbs.

'Kane told you to kill me, didn't he?' he sobbed.

'Yup.'

'He was scared I'd talk 'bout them telegraphs I sent. Wa'al, I won't. I swear I won't!'

'Nope, you sure won't,' agreed Delroy, unsheathing his Bowie knife.

Grainger scrambled unsteadily to his feet and backed off, his face white with fear. Delroy advanced towards him, the blood-lust showing all too clearly in his cold, black eyes. Grainger began to scream and made a desperate attempt to ward off the outlaw's blade. But he had no chance. His hands and arms were slashed to ribbons and then, with his defences beaten down, he suffered a vicious jab in the belly. The Bowie knife went in up to the hilt. Delroy grinned and, turning the knife in the wound, ripped the razor-sharp blade up through the croupier's body, lifting him bodily off the ground and hurling him backwards.

Grainger thumped into the trunk of a tree and slowly, almost gracefully, slid down the trunk.

He slumped there, in a sitting position, the huge knife buried deep in his body. His mouth hung open, blood trickling out of the corners and dripping onto his white shirt. Not that that mattered much, for the shirt was already soaked in blood from navel to sternum. The eyes remained open, but stared sightlessly up at his killer.

Spence Delroy dragged the lifeless body of Rick Grainger into the heart of the small wood and left him there. Then, pausing only to clean his knife, he climbed once more into the saddle and, leading Joe Grout's chestnut gelding, set off back in the direction of Red Rock.

It was five minutes past eight when, eventually, he rode into town and reined in the mare in front of Nat Baker's Eating-house. He dismounted, hitched the two horses to the rail outside and entered the eating-house. It was a long, narrow restaurant, containing two rows of a dozen or more small tables, all covered in red and white check tablecloths. Two of these tables had been pushed together in one corner and places laid for five persons. The Grout brothers and Travis Miller were already ensconced in this corner and Nat Baker was busily taking their orders. Delroy joined them and added his order to the others'.

'Did you take care of the croupier?' enquired Joe Grout, once the restaurateur had retired to the kitchen.

"Course I did,' growled Delroy.

'So, what now?' asked Tom Grout.

'We proceed accordin' to Norton's plan,' said Delroy.

'You reckon his hot-shot lawyer'll mebbe git him off?' said Sam Grout.

'Nope.'

'Then, we're gonna be needed,' said Miller.

'That's what I figure.'

'I'm lookin' forward to ridin' with Norton agin. He sure knew how to plan a job, whether it was a bank raid or a stage hold-up, or whatever. We was one helluva successful outfit with him as our leader,' said Joe Grout.

'Yeah, wa'al, let's keep our mouths shut 'bout that. Walls have ears, y'know,' said Miller, glancing nervously towards the kitchen.

Delroy nodded and added, 'Travis is right. Till we lam outa this one-horse town, we keep our heads down an' do nuthin' to excite anybody's suspicion.'

The others took this warning to heart and the conversation turned to how they had fared at the Golden Garter. Travis Miller and the two younger Grouts all boasted about their nights spent with Dan Evans' girls, while Joe Grout bewailed his ill luck at the poker table. It was while Spence Delroy was describing his small successes with the roulette wheel that Nat Baker reappeared bearing a couple of plates laden with bacon and eggs and potato cakes. The rest of the food quickly followed and the five desperadoes tucked in with gusto. The bacon and eggs were succeeded by pancakes oozing with honey, and all this was washed down with copious mugs of coffee. Breakfast at Nat Baker's wasn't just a meal; it was a feast.

They were drinking their fourth mug of coffee when Sheriff Luke Tanner entered the eating-house and walked slowly across to their corner. Spence Delroy smiled widely at the short, elderly figure standing before them. But there was no laughter in his cold, black eyes.

'You boys rode into town last night, I b'lieve?' said Tanner.

'Yup,' was Delroy's monosyllabic response.

'You got some business hereabouts?'

'An' if'n we did?' There was an edge to Joe Grout's voice.

'I'd like to know what it is. No offence, boys, but I'm the law in Red Rock, an' I like to keep tabs on any strangers who happen to stop over,' explained Tanner.

'That's all right, Sheriff,' said Travis Miller, hastily seeking to defuse the situation. 'We ain't got nuthin' to hide. Me an' my pardner, we figure on attendin' this here trial yo're holdin'.'

'Oh, yeah? An' what's this trial to you?'

'We once knew the accused. Rode together on a cattle drive, all the way up the Chisholm Trail from Texas.'

'So, yo're friends of his, huh?'

'No, I wouldn't say that. Didn't really care for the feller, to tell the truth. But we're interested, seein' as how we once knew him.'

'That's right, Sheriff. We figure on ridin' outa town jest as soon as the trial's over,' added Delroy.

Luke Tanner weighed up the two men. He didn't like what he saw. Having been told by Jack Stone that they were both killers and outlaws, Tanner was anxious to be rid of them as soon as possible. He reflected that, if they were telling the truth, he would, in fact, see the back of them before the day was out, for he considered it unlikely that the trial would run into a second day. He turned his attention to the Grout brothers.

'An' you boys, what's brought you to Red Rock?' he demanded.

Joe Grout smiled and replied in an even tone, 'Me an' my brothers are headin' for Kansas City. We're jest passin' through, is all.'

'So, you won't be stayin' for the trial,' said the sheriff pointedly.

Joe Grout took the hint.

'Nope,' he said mildly. 'As soon as we finish our coffee, we intend ridin' on out.'

'Fine!' Luke Tanner viewed the five men with a curious eye. Were they telling the truth, he wondered, or were they, as Jack Stone suspected, up to something? He prayed that Stone was wrong. 'See you two in court,' he said to Delroy and Miller. Then he turned and walked out of the restaurant.

His departure left the outlaws in some disarray.

'Why in tarnation did you say we was leavin' as

soon as we finish our coffee?' asked Tom Grout testily.

'What else could I say?' retorted his brother.

'Wa'al, so much for us waitin' in Flanagan's for the verdict!'

'The sheriff's gonna be tied up with the trial. He won't know whether we've left town or not.'

'An', if there's a break for lunch, which is quite likely, an' he strolls over to Flanagan's?' said Sam Grout.

'That could prove tricky. But s'pose we say. ...'

At this point, Travis Miller interrupted Joe Grout.

'There's a deserted homestead half a mile outa town. We passed it on the way in,' he said. 'You boys best hole up there. I reckon I could reach you an' we could ride back into town long 'fore the jury announce their verdict. Then, if'n we hitch up our hosses back of the stage line depot, they'll be real handy for our getaway.'

Joe Grout nodded thoughtfully. He stared across the eating-house and out through the window. The law office was directly opposite, with the Court House on one side and the stage line depot on the other.

'It depends on how quickly the jury arrive at their verdict,' he muttered.

'Hell, they're sure to take, at the very least, a quarter of an hour to twenty minutes! That's plenty of time for me to reach you, an' for us all to git back an' break into the law office!' retorted Miller.

'I agree,' said Delroy firmly.

Joe Grout pondered this for some moments.

'Wa'al, I s'pose so. Okay, we'll ride out to that homestead an' wait for you there,' he said finally.

'Right, let's finish our coffee. Then me an' Travis'll head for the Court House,' said Delroy, adding as an afterthought, "Fore you fellers ride outa town, be sure an' pick up some provisons, for it's gonna be a long ride to Nebraska.'

While Norton Kane's confederates were revising their plan of campaign, people were arriving in town for the trial. They came on horseback and in buckbords, rigs and buggies. Among the first of those to arrive were Jim Pelham and his wife, together with his foreman Ned Baines, and two of his oldest hands. All four men were wearing six-guns, a fact which did not please Luke Tanner, as he watched them from the doorway of the law office. The town ordinance against the carrying of firearms applied only to Saturday nights, yet he felt distinctly uneasy.

'I hope Jim don't do nuthin' stupid,' he growled.

'Why should he? I 'speck he's only come to see justice done,' drawled Stone.

The Kentuckian had called to enquire what the sheriff had gleaned from his interview with Spence Delroy and his pals, and neither he nor Johnnie Reid, Tanner's young, frank-faced deputy, had been at all reassured by what Tanner had told them.

'I still gotta feelin' them fellers is up to no good,'

said Stone, as Tanner left the doorway and stepped back into the office.

'But what in hell can they be plannin'?' asked the sheriff, scratching his head.

'Dunno.'

'Mebbe they're aimin' to raid the bank while everybody's at the trial?' suggested Johnnie Reid.

'That's possible, I s'pose,' mused Tanner.

'But unlikely,' said Stone.

'Why unlikely?' demanded the deputy.

"Cause they're gonna need someone to open the safe for 'em. An', as I recall, Garfield Tills said he was closin' the bank for the day. So, if'n they break in, there'll be nobody there with the keys to the safe,' explained Stone.

'They could mebbe use dynamite to blow it open?' said Tanner.

'You need a certain expertise to blow open a safe with dynamite,' replied the Kentuckian. 'An' even supposin' they do have that expertise, which I somehow doubt, the explosion would alert the whole darned town. They'd never git away with it.'

'Guess not,' said Tanner. 'So, what are they up to?'

'Mebbe nuthin' here in Red Rock. I'm convinced they're up to some kinda mischief, but it could be they're plannin' it some place else an' have merely rendezvoused here.'

'Wa'al, let's hope so.'

As Luke Tanner expressed this hope, Kitty from the Golden Garter stepped in through the open doorway. She was looking extremely attractive, dressed in her best blue velvet gown and matching bonnet. But there was a worried frown creasing her lily-white brow. Johnnie Reid stared at her voluptuous figure with a decidedly amorous eye, while Luke Tanner asked her what she wanted.

'I want to report a disappearance,' she replied.

'A disappearance! Whaddya mean? Who's disappeared?'

'Rick.'

'Rick Grainger?'

'The same. He ain't nowheres to be found.'

'Wa'al, he's a grown man an'. ...'

'There's somethin' wrong. I know it.'

'But, Kitty, a man like Rick. ...'

'He said he was gonna escort me to this here trial. Naturally, we was interested 'cause. ...'

'Jest git to the point, Kitty. Me 'n' Johnnie have to take Kane round to the Court House in 'bout five minutes,' said Tanner irritably.

'Yeah, wa'al, the point is, Rick didn't turn up.'

'So, mebbe he overslept?'

'Nope. I checked.'

'He could be with one of the other girls. Have you thought of that?'

''Course I have, an' he ain't. An' Dan Evans don't know where he is neither. I tell you, he's plain vanished into thin air.'

'That is a li'l strange, I'll grant you,' said Tanner.

'It's more 'n strange. It's spooky. I tell you,

Sheriff, somethin' jest ain't right. He was real anxious to attend the trial, so why would he take off without a word to nobody? An' why promise to escort me if he didn't mean to?'

'I'm afraid I cain't answer yore questions, Kitty. An' I cain't go lookin' for Rick neither, leastways not until after the trial.'

'I s'pose not. But you will look for him as soon as you can, won't yuh?' said Kitty anxiously.

'If Rick ain't re-appeared by the time the trial's over, I promise you I'll investigate,' stated Tanner.

Kitty had to be content with this promise, for the time had come for the sheriff and his deputy to march Norton Kane from his cell to the Court House by way of the rear doors. As the two lawmen vanished through the oak door leading to the cells, Kitty turned and stepped out into Main Street. Stone promptly followed the girl and, catching up with her, took her by the arm.

'Let me escort you, Miss Kitty,' he said gallantly.

'Why thank you, sir,' she replied, immediately cheered by the attention of the tall, broad-shouldered Kentuckian.

Stone, for his part, was also curious about the croupier's disappearance. His instincts coincided with those of the saloon girl. How in hell could anyone vanish in so small a town as Red Rock? Unless he had quit town? But, as Kitty had said, why would Rick Grainger do that when he seemed so anxious to witness Norton Kane's trial?

The Kentuckian was still pondering on this mystery when they joined the queue of people filing into the Court House.

EIGHT

Anybody who was anybody in and around Red Rock was present at the trial of Norton Kane. The front two rows of seats in the Court House had been reserved for the witnesses and the two newspapermen from Dodge City and Abilene. Immediately behind sat a stony-faced Jim Pelham, together with his wife and Ned Baines on one side and his two ranch hands on the other. In the same row were his fellow rancher, Les Gates, and his wife and two sons, while at one end of that row sat Ben Beardsley and his father-in-law, the Reverend John Dwyer. At the opposite end were the bank manager Garfield Tills and his wife, both eagerly awaiting the commencement of the trial.

Other notables, such as Doc Brady, the hotel owner Harry Lewin, Frank Flanagan, Dan Evans and that provider of gargantuan breakfasts, Nat Baker, were also present. They sat further back, while in the rearmost row were Felix Oates the mortician, and Spence Delroy and Travis Miller. Two rows in front of, and to one side of the two outlaws, sat Jack Stone and Kitty. The Kentuckian glanced over his shoulder at the outlaws, but they did not seem to have noticed him. Their eyes were fixed on the man in the dock.

Stone reverted his gaze to Norton Kane. The slim, thin-faced gunslinger was totally impassive. He did not appear in the least concerned with the excitement his case was causing. Indeed, he seemed to be quite oblivious of the hubbub in the Court House. Nor did the venomous stares of Jim Pelham and his men disturb his evident equanimity. He waited quietly, patiently, for the trial to commence. Flanking him, Sheriff Luke Tanner and his deputy looked a great deal less relaxed. They would not feel entirely happy until the verdict had been reached and Kane was once more safely locked up in his cell.

At nine o'clock sharp, the clerk of the court ushered in the judge. Jeremiah Hood had removed his stove-pipe hat and was attired in his robes of office. He cut an impressive figure, tall and imposing and sombre as an owl. He loomed large over the packed court and scoured it with an inquisitorial eye. Then he sat down and proceeded to swear in the jury. Those chosen were all solid citizens of Red Rock, none of whom had any known connection with the Bar Q ranch. The defence attorney made one or two objections, but, much to his displeasure, Judge Hood over-ruled him in peremptory fashion. Finally, all twelve were sworn in and the trial began.

Jack Stone watched with interest the performances of the two protagonists. Both lawyers were excellent orators, each capable of making the best of his case. Their styles, though, were quite dissimilar. Steve Morris, young and ambitious, stated the prosecution case with passion and conviction, and his examination of the witnesses was worthy of the Spanish Inquisition. Hiram Nettleton, on the other hand, conducted the defence in a much more restrained and relaxed manner. His questions, however, were no less pointed, even although they were put to the witnesses quietly and without rancour.

Norton Kane was called to the witness box by his advocate and gave a good account of himself. Nettleton led him gently through the night of Bobby McCoy's murder, laying heavy emphasis upon the fact that Bobby was wearing a gun. Kane did not deny that it was he who had called out the youngster, but he steadfastly refused to admit that Bobby McCoy was unarmed when the fatal shots were fired. Even Steve Morris's relentless cross-examination failed to shake Kane on this point.

The lawyers' closing speeches were deferred by Judge Jeremiah Hood until after lunch. The examination and cross-examination of the witnesses had taken most of the morning, and the court adjourned at ten minutes to twelve. It was set to reconvene at one o'clock precisely.

Jack Stone was quick to follow Spence Delroy and Travis Miller out of the Court House. He watched them stroll off along Main Street in the direction of Flanagan's Saloon. The Kentuckian turned to his fair companion.

'Wa'al, Miss Kitty, would you care for somethin' to eat?' he asked. Kitty smiled up at him.

'I wouldn't say no,' she replied.

'Okay, let's grab us a bite at Flanagan's,' suggested Stone.

The food at Flanagan's was by no means the best in town. It was, after all, a saloon rather than a restaurant. Nevertheless, Stone and the girl lunched reasonably well on hash and beans, washed down with several glasses of beer. Kitty, who was by nature a chatty soul, did most of the talking over lunch. This allowed the taciturn Kentuckian to concentrate on observing the two outlaws. Not that there was much to observe. They had little or no conversation and simply stood at the bar, drinking and smoking. Of the Grout brothers there was no sign. This should have reassured Stone, but it did not. His instincts told him that they were up to no good, and his instincts rarely let him down.

The trial recommenced upon the stroke of one, and the two advocates straightaway proceeded to make their final speeches. Both went carefully through the train of events leading up to Bobby McCoy's death, but came to quite different conclusions.

Hiram Nettleton concluded his speech by saying, 'And so, gentlemen of the jury, it comes down to this: nobody actually witnessed the shooting. Therefore, nobody can say with any degree of certainty that Bobby McCoy was *not* wearing a gun. I maintain there exists a reasonable doubt. Consequently, it is incumbent upon you, as honest, fair-minded citizens, to give my client the benefit of that reasonable doubt and find him not guilty. I rest my case.'

For his part, Steve Morris, the hawk-faced young state prosecutor, wound up his case by stating passionately, 'Although nobody witnessed the actual killing, I declare that there is no reasonable doubt whatsoever. Bobby McCoy was left-handed. It is inconceivable that he would have worn a hand-gun on his right thigh and drawn it with his right hand. Ergo, it must have been planted on him. And the only person who could possibly have done this was his killer, a man mortified by the beating he had earlier received at Bobby's hands. Norton Kane knew that Bobby McCoy was prohibited by a town ordinance from carrying a gun in Red Rock, on a Saturday night, and so, determined as he was to extract revenge, he contrived this clever plot in order to save himself from a charge of murder. He would have succeeded too, gentlemen of the jury, had Bobby, like the vast majority of us, been right-handed. I am sure, however, that you will not let this patent subterfuge divert you from your duty. You will, you must, find Norton Kane guilty of the cold-blooded murder of Bobby McCoy!'

Following the two closing speeches, Judge Jeremiah Hood summed up. He was succinct and to the point, and came as near as he dared to

directing the jury to find Norton Kane guilty. Then
he ordered them to retire to consider their verdict.

At this juncture, Stone chanced to glance behind
him and, in consequence, observed Travis Miller
rise and slip quietly out of the Court House. The
Kentuckian's suspicions were immediately further
aroused. For what reason, he asked himself, would
Miller leave the trial *before* the verdict was
announced? While he sat awaiting the return of
the jury, he endeavoured to come up with an
answer to this mystery. But no answer came. Stone
was still wrestling with this enigma when the jury
filed back into the courtroom.

Judge Hood addressed them in sombre tones.

'Have you reached your verdict?' he demanded.

'Yes, yore honour, we have,' stated the foreman.

'And is it unanimous?'

'It is, yore honour.'

'Wa'al, tell the court what it is.'

'We find the defendant guilty as charged.'

This pronouncement produced a raucous mixture of gleeful yells, shouts of approval and angry
demands that Norton Kane should be strung up
without delay. The judge patiently waited some
minutes for the furore to die down a little and then,
with the aid of his gavel, brought the court to order.

He faced the defendant, who, Stone noted, had
shown no emotion whatsoever when the jury's
verdict was announced. Judge Hood looked even
more severe than usual and, when he spoke, it was
in a voice of thunder.

'Norton Kane,' he boomed, 'you have been found

guilty of the most heinous crime, that of murdering one of your fellow-men. I have no compunction, therefore, in sentencing you to death. You will be taken from this place and, as soon as may conveniently be arranged, hanged by the neck until you are dead. May God have mercy on your soul. Amen!'

Hood's judgment produced further shouting and cheering and, in the second row, Les Gates could be seen happily shaking Jim Pelham by the hand, while Ned Baines and his fellow ranch hands were slapping one another on the back and throwing their hats in the air. Indeed, everyone, with the single exception of the impassive prisoner, seemed overjoyed at the result. Bobby McCoy had been a popular youngster and the good people of Red Rock were delighted to see justice done.

Although she had liked Kane and had not approved of Bobby McCoy's assault upon him, Kitty had nonetheless been appalled at the retribution exacted by the gunslinger. Now she was happy that he had been convicted, and she expressed her happiness by throwing her arms round Jack Stone's neck and kissing him. In normal circumstances, Stone would not have objected, for Kitty was a most attractive young woman. However, at that moment, he had other things on his mind. Therefore, he freed himself from her embraces with as much speed as politeness would permit. But he was too late. By the time he glanced again towards the rearmost

row, Spence Delroy had vanished. Stone cursed
beneath his breath.

'Say, Jack, somethin' bitin' you? Ain't you glad
that sonofabitch is gonna git his just deserts?'
asked the girl.

'Shuddup!' he snapped.

'Now, lookee here, I don't have to. ...'

'Shuddup!'

Kitty shut up. The look on the Kentuckian's
face warned her that he was not to be argued
with. He was furious with himself. He knew now
what Delroy and the others were planning. It had
been so obvious, he could not believe he had failed
to rumble it earlier. The mysterious disappearance of the croupier, Rick Grainger, should
have given him a clue.

He had bumped into Grainger in Plainville, and
Grainger had told him he was over there
conducting some private business. That private
business, Stone concluded, had been the sending
of telegraphs to summon Spence Delroy and his
friends to Red Rock. And, Stone further concluded, the telegraphs had been sent on behalf of
Grainger's erstwhile star customer, Norton Kane.
Which would account for Grainger's sudden
disappearance. His usefulness had ended and, as
far as Kane was concerned, he knew too much.
Stone guessed that his old acquaintance had gone
the way of Bobby McCoy.

Travis Miller's and then Spence Delroy's
departure from the courtroom told him all he
needed to know. They had been waiting for the

verdict before they made their move.

Stone peered over the heads of the crowd towards the box in which Norton Kane had stood, flanked by the sheriff and his deputy. All three were in the process of leaving the Court House, prior to returning to the law office. Stone tried yelling a warning, but could not make himself heard above the general hubbub. Haplessly, he watched as the two lawmen and their prisoner left through the rear door of the Court House.

Turning and pushing past Kitty, Stone forced his way through the jostling crowd and out into Main Street. As he reached the sidewalk, he was just in time to see the rear end of a horse disappear down the alleyway between the law office and the stage line depot. Pulling the Frontier Model Colt from his holster, the Kentuckian left the sidewalk and began running down the parallel alleyway that ran between the Court House and the law office.

The unlocked door should have warned him.

'Hell, I could've sworn I locked this 'fore we went to court!' exclaimed Sheriff Luke Tanner, as he pushed open the door and shoved Kane into the narrow passage beyond.

'It looks to me as though the lock's been tampered with,' said Johnnie Reid.

'That's right, sonny. It has.'

The door leading into the office swung open and Spence Delroy emerged, his gun trained on Tanner. At the same instant, Joe Grout appeared behind Johnnie Reid and dealt him a vicious blow to the back of the skull with the barrel of his revolver. The deputy slumped to the ground and Luke Tanner opened his mouth to yell.

'I wouldn't if I was you,' snarled Delroy, stepping quickly forward and jabbing his Remington into the sheriff's open mouth.

'Okay, git me outa these goddam handcuffs!' snapped Kane, for Tanner had handcuffed the prisoner's hands behind his back prior to escorting him back to the cells.

'Where's the key?' demanded Delroy, removing the Remington from the sheriff's mouth.

'Go to hell!' retorted Tanner defiantly.

Delroy smiled a sinister smile and began pistol-whipping the lawman. He set about this task with sadistic glee. A series of swift, vicious blows split both the lawman's eyebrows and smashed his nose into a pulp. Tanner gasped with pain and fell onto his knees, his face a mask of dripping blood.

'The keys are in his vest pocket,' said Kane.

'You spoilt my fun, Norton. I wanted him to tell me,' drawled Delroy and, with one last tremendous blow, he laid Luke Tanner out cold.

Then grinning wickedly, he knelt down beside the sheriff and extracted the key from Tanner's vest pocket.

By the time Delroy had set Kane free and he and Joe Grout had managed to drag the senseless bodies of the sheriff and his deputy into one of the cells, the others appeared at the rear door with six horses, all saddled and ready to ride. The keys to the cell-doors had been left hanging in the door of the cell previously occupied by Kane, and it was in this cell that the two lawmen were dumped. Kane took and strapped on the sheriff's gun-belt, complete with Colt Peacemaker, and then turned and carefully locked the cell-door.

'Guess we'll take these keys with us,' he said.

'Yeah. Why not?' laughed Joe Grout.

'Anyways, boys, I'm mighty glad to see y'all,' said Kane. 'Gotta thank you for comin' an' gittin' me outa this mess.'

'Wa'al, it'll be jest like old times with you to lead us,' said Joe Grout.

'Sure will,' added Travis Miller from the open doorway. 'You plan a few successful raids, like you did in the past, an' that'll be thanks enough.'

'That's right,' said Delroy. 'But, for Chrissake, let's quit gabbin' an' git the hell outa here!'

Norton Kane nodded. He, for one, was extremely anxious to shake off the dust of Red Rock for the last time.

'Okay. Let's go,' he said.

The first three to mount were Tom and Sam Grout and Travis Miller. The rest were half-way between the law office and where the horses stood when, all of a sudden, Jack Stone erupted from the alleyway next to the Court House.

The Kentuckian's first shot toppled Sam Grout out of the saddle, while his second struck Travis Miller in the chest and likewise knocked him clean off his horse. Returning fire, Tom Grout hurriedly dismounted and retreated towards the law office. A third shot whipped the Stetson from his head as, in his haste to find cover, he collided with his elder brother. The two Grouts cannoned into Norton Kane, who, in turn, staggered backwards and fell against Spence Delroy. Crouching in the alleyway, Stone's fourth and fifth shots sent the four men scuttling for the shelter of the law office.

Sam Grout, meantime, clambered unsteadily to his feet and, clutching his shoulder, made a dash for cover. He was quickly followed By Travis Miller, the latter with blood oozing from a huge hole in his chest. The colour had left Miller's face and, as he ran, he coughed up large mouthfuls of crimson blood. Despite his terrible wound, however, he still managed to cover the ground in long strides. Then, as he reached the open doorway of the law office, he turned to fire at the Kentuckian. And so it was that he, rather than Sam Grout, fell victim to Stone's sixth and final bullet. The forty-five calibre slug hit him plumb between the eyes and blasted his brains out through the back of his skull.

The shooting had naturally enough attracted the attention of the rest of the population and a number of Red Rock's citizenry hurried down the alleyway in the wake of the Kentuckian. Among the first to arrive upon the scene were Jim Pelham, Les Gates and his sons, Ned Baines and Pelham's two ranch hands.

'What in tarnation's goin' on?' demanded

Pelham, as he observed Stone standing in the alleyway, calmly reloading his Frontier Model Colt.

'Some of Kane's friends tried to spring him,' replied the Kentuckian. 'There's one dead an' another winged,' he added.

Pelham eyed the corpse of Travis Miller, lying a few feet away from the rear door of the law office.

'In there, are they?' he growled.

'Yup.'

'What about the sheriff an' young Johnnie Reid?' enquired Ben Beardsley who, together with Doc Brady and Harry Lewin, had by now joined Stone and the others.

'Reckon they was taken by surprise,' said Stone.

'So, they're holed up in there with Kane and his pals?' said the mayor.

'Guess so.'

'Dead or alive?' asked Doc Brady.

'Dunno. Alive, I hope.'

'What're we gonna do? Could we mebbe rush 'em?' suggested Jim Pelham.

Stone laughed harshly.

'An' git ourselves killed?' he rasped.

'Wa'al, whaddya suggest, then,' snapped Ned Baines.

'We surround the law office so's there ain't no way out for Kane an' his gang. An' then we jest sit an' wait,' said Stone.

'We cain't wait forever,' Pelham pointed out.

'Nope. But let's do as Mr Stone suggests. Once we got the bastards pinned down, then we can discuss what to do next,' said Les Gates.

Pelham carefully considerd this proposal from the owner of the Lazy S. He had to admit that it made sound sense.

'Okay, let's do jest that,' he said finally.

Thereupon, it was agreed that Stone should organise a tight net round Red Rock's law office. This the Kentuckian did without further delay. Les Gates and his two sons covered the law office's rear door from the alley between it and the Court House, while Jim Pelham, Ned Baines and the other two from the Bar Q covered it from the next alley. The front was also covered. Half a dozen men crouched in Ned Baker's Eating-house opposite, all armed with Winchesters, and there were more armed men in the shops on either side of the restaurant. An uncanny silence fell upon that part of town, although crowds had gathered both inside and outside Flanagan's Saloon and the Golden Garter, where they hung about eagerly discussing this unforeseen turn of events.

Another rather more formal discussion took place inside the Court House. Judge Jeremiah Hood presided and those present consisted of Ben Beardsley, his father-in-law and his fellow councillors, Doc Brady and Jack Stone. The thorny question was how to effect the safe release of Luke Tanner and Johnnie Reid.

In the end, it was decided that the only way was to offer Kane and his men their freedom in exchange for the lives of the sheriff and his deputy. Nobody, least of all the judge, was particularly happy with this solution. But it seemed to be the only one available to them.

'Jim Pelham won't like it,' said Doc Brady darkly.

'Hell, I don't like it!' exclaimed the judge.

'You weren't close to Bobby McCoy like Jim was. He treated that boy almost like a son,' said Garfield Tills.

'So, we sacrifice Luke 'n' Johnnie jest to satisfy Jim's thirst for revenge!' rasped Beardsley.

'You gonna tell him, then, Ben?' asked Doc Brady.

The mayor grimaced and shrugged his shoulders.

'Guess so,' he said.

'I'll go fetch him,' said Stone.

'Okay, we'll meet you in Nat Baker's place,' said Judge Hood. 'Then, we shall be in position to shout across the street with our offer.'

It was some minutes before they all regrouped in the eating-house, for they had to circle round and enter it from the rear. The last to arrive were the Kentuckian and the rancher.

'Mr Stone here tells me you gotta plan,' said Pelham, as he joined the others.'So, whaddya reckon on doin'?' he demanded.

Quietly and slowly, Ben Beardsley told him what they had in mind. When he had finished, the rancher stared at him and, for what seemed a veritable age, said absolutely nothing. Then, all at once, he exploded.

'You yeller-livered skunks, yo're tellin' me that

yo're proposin' to let that murderin', no-account critter escape scot-free?' he cried furiously.

Judge Hood eyed him coldly.

'I ain't yeller-livered,' he snapped.

'Then, why …?'

'It was no easy decision. But what's the alternative?'

'Like I said earlier, we could storm the law office.'

'We'd be sittin' ducks. Those murderin' varmints'd massacre us as sure as eggs is eggs.'

'We'd subdue 'em in the end.'

'At the cost of how many lives, for Chrissake?' said Stone. 'Five? Ten? Fifteen? Twenty? You really b'lieve it'd be worth that?'

'Think about it, Jim,' said Beardsley. 'Jest think about it.'

The rancher scowled. He dearly wanted vengeance. But, as he considered what the judge and Stone had said, he reluctantly came to the conclusion that, however unpalatable it might be, their plan was the only one that made any kind of sense.

'Okay,' he growled. 'Make 'em yore goddam offer!'

'You'll go along with it?' said the judge.

'I s'pose.'

Jeremiah Hood smiled thinly. He crossed the dining-room and crouched down beneath the open window. Cautiously, he raised his head. Opposite, the law office looked deserted. But he knew it was not, and that any shots aimed towards it would draw an instant response from the outlaws.

'Kane, can you hear me?' he cried.

'I can hear you,' came the immediate response, although Kane wisely kept his head down.

'This is Judge Hood speakin'.'

'Okay. So, whaddya gotta say?'

'I think we can do a deal.'

'A deal?'

'Yes. Yore freedom for the lives of the sheriff an' his deppity. I take it that they are both still alive?'

'You take it right, Judge.'

'Wa'al, whaddya say?'

'Okay. But, jest so's there ain't no renegin' on yore part, I reckon we'll take the deppity along as a hostage. We'll release him as soon as we cross the state line.'

'Now, lookee here. ...'

'That's my final word.'

'Goddam it, I cain't agree to that!'

'Think it over, Judge.'

'But. ...'

'I'll give you one hour. If'n you ain't agreed by then, reckon I'll have to give you a li'l encouragement by shootin' Sheriff Tanner.'

Judge Hood returned to where the others sat, morosely grouped round a couple of Nat Baker's gaily-bedecked tables. Ben Beardsley was the first to speak.

'I guess we got no choice but to go along with Kane's demands,' he sighed.

'Wa'al, I wouldn't trust that sonofabitch. What's the bettin' he kills Johnnie jest as soon as he's safely across the border into Nebraska?' said Doc Brady.

'Johnnie won't be goin'. I will,' said Beardsley.

'What are you sayin', Ben?' exclaimed the Reverend John Dwyer, looking askance at his son-in-law.

'I'm sayin' I bear some responsibility for the present situation. If I hadn't bank-rolled Kane, he would never have stayed on in Red Rock an' then....'

'But you owed the man. He once saved yore life. In the same circumstances, I'd've acted exactly as you did,' said the preacher.

'Would you? Wa'al, I ain't willin' to have another death on my conscience. So, Judge, you shout across to Kane an' tell him what we've decided. Reckon he'll happily settle to have me, the mayor of Red Rock, as his hostage.'

The judge did as Beardsley had bidden him, although the Reverend John Dwyer continued to protest, exhorting Beardsley to think of his wife and children. While Beardsley explained to his father-in-law that his honour demanded he stand in for Johnnie Reid, Kane, having agreed to the substitution, was making one final demand.

'One of my men is hit,' he yelled. 'So, 'fore we ride out, he'll need some attention. You send Doc Brady across, okay? I'll guarantee he comes to no harm.'

Judge Hood turned and looked at the doctor, whose normally ruddy complexion had become quite pale.

'You willin', Doc?' he asked.

Brady nodded, although he looked none too happy at the prospect.

'Okay,' shouted the judge. 'But, if anythin' should happen to the doc, the deal's off. Understood?'

'Understood, Judge.'

Ben Beardsley took the doctor by the arm and, pushing open the door of Nat Baker's establishment, stepped cautiously out into the street. Then he and Doc Brady walked slowly across to the law office and vanished inside. And, while the doctor was busily engaged in binding up Sam Grout's shoulder wound, the judge and Jim Pelham were issuing orders to the men surrounding the law office. They told them that Kane and his gang should be permitted to escape without hindrance. These orders were not well received. Ned Baines and his two pals, in particular, were reluctant to hold their fire, but, in the end, Jim Pelham persuaded them. He had given the judge his word and he, like Beardsley, was jealous of his honour. Consequently, half an hour later, Norton Kane, Spence Delroy and the three Grout brothers galloped away from Red Rock. And, to guarantee their safe passage, they had Ben Beardsley, his wrists bound in front of him and seated upon the late Travis Miller's sturdy bay gelding, riding in their midst.

NINE

Judge Jeremiah Hood viewed the fast-disappearing outlaws with blazing eyes. His face was as though carved from granite. He had been forced to agree to Norton Kane's terms. If he had not, both the sheriff and his deputy would have been murdered; of that he had no doubt. Yet it nettled him. He was supposed to uphold the law, not connive at its being thwarted.

The judge was not the only one to be enraged by the unfortunate turn of events. Jim Pelham was as mad as a bear in a pit. He turned to the judge and roared, 'So, the sonsofbitches have gotten theirselves safely outa town. Still, there's one helluva ride ahead of 'em 'fore they reach Nebraska!'

'What are you sayin'?' asked the judge.

'I'm sayin' we should swear up a posse an' git after 'em,' said the rancher.

'Let's go see the sheriff,' suggested Hood.

'Yeah, Jim, Luke's the man to lead us,' agreed Les Gates.

But, in the event, they found Luke Tanner to be

in no condition to lead anybody anywhere. He and Johnnie Reid lay unconscious in the cell recently vacated by Norton Kane. As Kane had ridden off with the keys, a search had to be made for duplicates. Eventually, these were found in the sheriff's office desk, and the first to enter the cell was Doc Brady. He crouched down beside the two lawmen and carefully examined them. Then he looked up at the judge and sadly shook his head.

'Cain't see either of 'em recoverin' consciousness for some li'l time,' he said. 'An', when they do, neither's gonna be fit to lead no posse. Leastways, not for a day or so, Luke, in partickler, has been beaten up pretty badly.'

'Hell, if'n we wait a day or so, those murderin' bastards'll be over the state line an' there'll be no catchin' 'em!' exclaimed Jim Pelham.

'Me an' my two boys, we're ready an' willin' to ride after them varmints right now,' said Les Gates.

'With me an' my men, that makes us seven,' said Pelham. 'So, who else will ride with us?'

But none of the townsfolk seemed at all keen. They had been prepared, from the cover of Red Rock's various stores and other establishments, to keep Kane and his gang pinned down in the law office. They were not, however, at all anxious to pursue the five outlaws across the wild and rugged terrain that lay between Red Rock and the border of Kansas and Nebraska. Judge Hood stated their fears for them.

'Kane an' his men are all professional gunslingers. Supposin' you do catch up with 'em, they'll outshoot you for sure. Goddam it, Jim, you an' yore boys are cowpokes not gunmen!'

'But what about Ben? We cain't jest leave him. ...' began Pelham.

'If'n you follow Kane an' his men an' they git wind of you, it's quite likely they'll shoot the mayor out of hand.'

'So, yo're sayin' we let 'em go?'

'I'm afraid so.'

'If we had a professional gunfighter to lead us. ...'

'That would be different.'

Jim Pelham slapped his thigh.

'Jack Stone!' he cried. 'Stone could lead us!'

However, of the Kentuckian there was no sign. He had entered the law office with the rest of them, and had been among the first to see the two lawmen lying senseless in the cell. While the others had been searching for the duplicate cell-keys, though, he had apparently slipped away.

Jack Stone headed south on the trail that would eventually lead him to Dodge City. Against his better judgement, he had involved himself in the recent events in Red Rock. Yet, despite his intervention, Norton Kane and his gang had succeeded in escaping. Well, he had done his best. It was no longer his concern. At least, this is what he told himself as he rode south.

He had left Judge Hood and the others in the

law office and had made his way to the livery
stables in South Street. There he had saddled up
his bay gelding, paid the ostler what he owed, and
ridden quietly out of town.

Now he was beginning to have doubts. While it
was really none of his business, nevertheless, he
had chosen to involve himself, and he had an
aversion to leaving business, any kind of business,
unfinished. Also, there was Ben Beardsley to
consider. Stone had to admit that the mayor's
chances of survival, once Kane and his gang
reached Nebraska, were pretty slim. Could he
therefore, in all conscience, leave Beardsley to his
fate? Reluctantly, he came to the conclusion that
he could not.

Slowly and unenthusiastically, Stone turned
the gelding's head and galloped back the way he
had come. He skirted Red Rock and headed
northwards. His experience as an Indian scout for
the US cavalry stood him in good stead, and he
soon picked up the trail of his quarry. Their tracks
were not difficult to follow, though he stalked the
outlaws with a fair degree of caution, for he had
no wish that they should spot him. If he were to
succeed in eliminating them and at the same time
freeing Ben Beardsley, he would need, at the very
least, an element of surprise.

Kane and his gang rode all through that night.
They breakfasted on the banks of the Solomon
River, which they afterwards forded. Apart from
this halt, they made only a couple of brief stops for
the sake of their horses. And, so, they succeeded

in crossing the state line into Nebraska as dusk was beginning to fall on the following evening.

Stone had by now caught up with them, and he watched as they entered the small Nebraskan settlement of Silver Gulch, half a mile north of the border. Silver Gulch had once been a bustling mining town, but the seams had run out and the people had left. In consequence, it was now merely a ghost town. The Kentuckian observed the five outlaws and their prisoner trot slowly up the main street. They reined in their horses in front of what was once Silver Gulch's one and only saloon, and promptly dismounted. Then, having hitched the horses to the rail outside the saloon, they trooped in through the batwing doors. Stone also dismounted and, crouching behind a tumble of boulders, on a ridge overlooking the town, he settled down to watch and wait. Not that there was much to see, apart from the tumbleweed gusting along the street, blown by the light evening breeze.

While the Kentuckian was watching the tumbleweed and wondering what to do next, Kane and the others were making themselves comfortable inside the deserted saloon. Tom Grout, before he had turned to a life of crime, had once served as a cook on a wagon train. Consequently, he was despatched to the kitchen with the gang's provisions, there to brew up some coffee and produce a meal. This was likely to take some little time and, in the meantime, Joe Grout tended to his youngest brother's wound.

'How is it, Sam?' enquired Norton Kane.

'It's hurtin' bad,' said Sam Grout. 'But a night's rest should help.'

'Yeah. Wa'al, there ain't no need for you to stir for a day or two. You an' the others can rest up here while I ride over to Franklin an' run an eye over the bank there,' drawled Kane.

Joe Grout's eyes glinted and he asked, 'You plannin' we should raid that there bank?'

'That's what I figure. Jest as soon as Sam's fit 'nough.'

Sam Grout winced as his brother removed the dressing from his wound.

'Hell, Norton, I reckon you'd best go ahead without me! I guess it's gonna be a week or two 'fore I'm likely to be much use to you,' he said.

'Wa'al, we'll wait 'n' see,' said Kane.

'An' … er … what about me?' enquired Ben Beardsley anxiously. 'Now yo're safely over the state line into Nebraska, you don't need me no more.'

'That's right, Ben; we don't,' said Kane.

'So, how's about lettin' me go?'

'I don't reckon we can do that, Ben.'

'Why not?'

''Cause you might take it into yore head to ride over to Lexington, an' drop in on the US marshals' office there.'

'I wouldn't, Kane! I swear I wouldn't!'

'No?'

'No; I'd head straight for home.'

'Wa'al, I'm afraid I cain't take that chance.'

'Aw, come on, Kane, you … you cain't mean to kill me, surely? We once shared a cell together an'. …'

Kane interrupted the mayor with a wave of his hand.

'That was a long while ago, Ben,' he said.

'But … but, look at the way I bank-rolled you back in Red Rock!'

'Sorry, Ben. This is nuthin' personal.' Kane turned to Spence Delroy and asked, 'Would you mind 'tendin' to this for me, Spence? I'd take it as a favour if'n you would.'

He had picked the right man for the job. Delroy's fingers tightened round the hilt of his Bowie knife and he grinned wolfishly.

'It'll be a pleasure, Norton,' he hissed, and he meant just that. For Spence Delroy, killing was always a pleasure.

'Take him outside, then,' said Kane.

'But don't jest gun him down in the street,' rasped Joe Grout, momentarily pausing in his ministrations.

'Why in tarnation shouldn't I gun him down in the street?' demanded Delroy.

''Cause you leave him lyin' out there an' he's gonna attract coyotes.'

'So? You ain't scared of coyotes, are yuh, Joe?'

'Nope, but I'm dog-tired an' I'm lookin' forward to a good night's sleep. An' you know how them darned coyotes can howl!'

'Joe's right,' said Kane. 'I observed some livery stables as we rode into town. Take Ben along there an' dump his body in one of them stables.'

Delroy nodded and, drawing his Remington from its holster, he prodded it into Beardsley's belly.

'No! No! You cain't do this!' cried Beardsley.

'I can an' I will,' snarled Delroy. 'Now, git goin'.'

'Start walkin', Ben, or he'll shoot you on the spot,' said Kane.

Beardsley gazed beseechingly at the outlaw leader, but Norton Kane had no intention of relenting. He had some regrets, for he had no grudge against the man and he thought that Beardsley probably did intend riding straight back to Red Rock. However, if he and his gang were to make the ghost town of Silver Gulch their hideaway, the Nebraskan lair from which they would ride out on a series of raids across the state, then he could not afford to take any chance, however slight, that Beardsley might betray their whereabouts. He returned the other's gaze and silently shook his head.

With the barrel of Delroy's revolver transferred from the pit of his belly to the small of his back, Ben Beardsley walked slowly, unwillingly, out through the batwing doors. He proceeded at a funereal pace down the main street towards the deserted livery stables, desperately scouring the empty buildings he passed, hoping to devise some means of escape. But no inspiration came and eventually the two men reached the stables. One of the main doors hung half-open, swaying and creaking in the light evening breeze.

'Inside,' snapped Delroy, giving the mayor a sharp jab with the gun.

Beardsley staggered forward and found himself in the centre of stables similar to those he owned back in Red Rock. Facing him, along the length of one wall, were a dozen or more stalls. A cold shiver ran down Beardsley's spine, as he contemplated the likelihood of his dead body being dumped in one of these stalls. He turned to face his would-be executioner.

'Look, gimme a break,' he begged. 'You could let me go. Kane an' the others need never know.'

Spence Delroy laughed. A harsh, mirthless laugh, the laugh of a human hyena. He slowly dropped the Remington back into its holster. Then he drew the huge, razor-sharp Bowie knife from its sheath.

'I ain't gonna shoot you,' he hissed. 'No, I'm gonna slice you up with this here Bowie knife. I tell yuh, there ain't nuthin' so enjoyable as killin' a man with a knife. It's so deliciously painful an' so deliciously slow. Yessir, I'm gonna jest love this!'

'No! For Chrissake! No!' Beardsley backed off, his eyes wide with horror and his mouth dry with fear. He was no coward, but the sight of the enormous, double-edged blade made his blood run cold. 'No!' he screamed.

'Yes,' said Delroy, and he jabbed viciously at his intended victim.

Beardsley leapt backwards avoiding the thrust by a mere hair's breadth. He was sweating profusely and the colour had faded from his face. He made an attempt to grapple with Delroy, but the outlaw was too quick for him and, as a result, he suffered a nasty gash on his right forearm, Delroy's formidable blade slashing through his jacket and shirt-sleeves and raking his flesh.

Excited by the sight of Beardsley's blood, Spence Delroy let loose a maniacal laugh and advanced upon the wounded man. His blade flashed yet again, but this time missed. However, in avoiding its thrust, Beardsley stumbled and fell. With the mayor now completely at his mercy, Delroy once again raised the Bowie knife.

The sound of the shot echoed throughout the empty stables. Spence Delroy staggered forward a couple of paces, whereupon the huge knife slipped from his grasp and he suddenly collapsed flat on his face in the dust. He twitched a few times, and then lay quite still. Beardsley glanced from the huge hole in the middle of Delroy's back to the smoking revolver in Jack Stone's right hand.

The Kentuckian stood framed in the open doorway. He had seen the two men walk from the saloon to the livery stables and had guessed what was about to happen. Therefore, he had immediately scrambled down from the ridge above the town and hurried across to the stables, as fast as his long legs would carry him. And he had made it in time. But only just in time.

'Jeez, am I pleased to see you!' exclaimed Beardsley.

'Figured you might be,' grinned Stone, dropping the Frontier Model Colt back into its holster. Then he saw the blood dripping from Beardsley's arm. 'Hey, yo're hurt!' he cried.

''Tain't nuthin',' protested Beardsley.

'It needs bandagin',' retorted Stone.

In the absence of anything better, the Kentuckian ripped the one unbloodied sleeve off the mayor's shirt, tore it into strips and used these to bind the wound. And, while he was thus engaged, he quietly answered the other's questions.

'Are you here on your own, Stone?' asked Beardsley.

'Yup.'

'I'd've thought a posse. ...'

'Who would've led 'em? Both the sheriff an' his deppity were out for the count.'

'Even so. ...'

'Jim Pelham wanted to form a posse. But I guess Judge Hood talked him out of it.'

'You guess?'

'I slipped away 'fore they'd finished their deliberations.'

'An' you trailed us all the way here?'

'It was easy enough.'

'Wa'al, I sure gotta thank you. It must've taken some guts comin' on after them murderin' sonsofbitches all on yore lonesome!'

Stone smiled grimly.

'I didn't do it jest for yore sake, Beardsley,' he drawled. 'I also did it for mine. I'm a man who's gotta see a thing through.'

'I'm mighty glad you have!' declared Beardsley. Then, he asked anxiously,, 'So, whaddya figure we should do now?'

'Now, we finish what I began.'

'Couldn't we jest slip away an' …?'

'You scared, Beardsley?'

'Wa'al, I ain't no gunslinger an' there's four of them agi'n the two of us.'

'You can handle a gun, cain't yuh?'

'Sure. But, like I said, I ain't that quick on the draw.'

'You won't have to be, for I ain't plannin' to call 'em out.'

'Nope?'

'Nope. I'm aimin' to give them the same chance that that bastard lyin' there was gonna give you. No chance at all.'

'I don't understand. …'

'Kane an' the others must've heard the shot an' figured Delroy has plugged you. So, they'll be expectin' him to saunter back into that saloon in a coupla minutes. Therefore, we have the advantage of surprise, an', I tell you, we're gonna use it. When we walk through them batwing doors, we don't give 'em no kinda warnin'. We walk in with our guns blazin'.'

'I ain't got no gun.'

Stone smiled and, bending down beside the corpse of Spence Delroy, removed the dead man's Remington from its holster. Then, he straightened up and handed the gun to Beardsley. And, while Beardsley examined the Remington, the Kentuckian drew his Frontier Model Colt and carefully slipped a sixth bullet into the recently emptied chamber.

'Okay?' he said.

Beardsley nodded.

The two men stepped outside. The light was continuing to fade. In another half-hour or so it would be dark.

'We'd better git movin',' said Stone. 'We gotta finish this while we can still see what we're doin'.'

They quickened their pace, hurrying through the drifting tumbleweed until they came abreast of the saloon. Then they clattered up the short flight of wooden steps onto the stoop. Beardsley was clutching the Remington in his right hand and, as they approached the doorway of the saloon, Stone promptly drew his Frontier Model Colt.

'Okay, here we go,' he whispered, and the two men pushed open the batwing doors and marched into the derelict saloon.

TEN

The three gunmen would have had no warning whatsoever had it not been that Tom Grout chose that very moment to emerge from the kitchen, bearing a pot of coffee.

'Jeez, look out!' he yelled, throwing down the coffee-pot and making a grab for his revolver.

As he shouted, so Norton Kane and Joe Grout turned. Joe Grout had just finished bandaging his brother's wound, while Kane had been examining one of the saloon's lamps to see if it contained any kerosene. They whirled round, their faces perfect studies of shocked disbelief. But, before they could even reach for their guns, Beardsley and the Kentuckian opened fire.

Beardsley had no compunction in gunning down the man who had so callously attempted to send him to his death. It was no thanks to Kane that Spence Delroy hadn't cut him to pieces. His first shot struck the outlaw in the left shoulder and spun him round. Kane fell sideways, crashed into a card table and toppled to the floor. Upon hitting the boards, Kane rolled over and, snatching from

its holster the Colt Peacemaker, which he had
taken off Sheriff Luke Tanner's senseless body, he
returned fire. But his shot was hurried and it
missed its mark. Beardsley's second shot, on the
other hand, did not. It blasted a hole in the outlaw's
belly the size of a dinner plate. Kane dropped his
gun and fell back against the overturned table. He
clutched his belly in a desperate effort to prevent
his guts from spilling out all over the floor. As he
did so, Beardsley's third shot drilled a neat hole in
his forehead and exploded out of the back of his
skull, sending an odious mixture of bone-splinters,
blood and brains splattering through the air.

While Ben Beardsley was devoting all of his
attention to Norton Kane, Jack Stone was coldly
and dispassionately disposing of the three Grout
brothers.

The Kentuckian's first shot struck Joe Grout, as
he turned upon hearing his brother's warning
shout. The bullet entered his left ear and lodged in
his brain, killing him instantly. He crashed to the
floor, cannoning into Sam Grout as he did so. The
youngest Grout yelled in pain, for his brother had
unfortunately made contact with his injured
shoulder. It was the last sound that Sam Grout
ever uttered. Stone's second shot hit him in the
throat. He gurgled up a large quantity of crimson
blood and, clutching at his throat, sank to his
knees. A third shot from the Kentuckian's gun
blasted a huge hole in his chest and threw him onto
his back, where he lay dying and slowly coughing
up the remains of his life's blood.

Of the three brothers, only Tom Grout succeeded in drawing his gun. But his shot, like Norton Kane's, was hurried. Stone felt the wind of it on his left cheek. He grinned and, carefully aiming the Frontier Model Colt at the last surviving outlaw, squeezed the trigger. The forty-five calibre slug tore through bone and gristle, smashing Tom Grout's rib-cage and slicing through his heart. He was thrown a good six feet backwards and ended up spreadeagled on the floor, half-way through the doorway leading into the kitchen.

The two men stood and surveyed the scene. The action in the saloon had taken place in less than a minute and, at the end of it, four men lay dead upon the floor. Beardsley gazed at the corpses in astonishment. He could scarcely believe that Kane and his gang had all perished while he remained on his feet, quite unscathed apart from the earlier knife-wound. He turned to the Kentuckian and exclaimed, with a wry grin, 'Goddam it, Stone, that was some shoot-out!'

'Yup.' Stone dropped his revolver into its holster and, slapping the mayor on the back, said cheerfully, 'Wa'al, reckon you can go home now.'

'Er … yeah. You … you ridin' along?'

'Guess so, though I won't be callin' in at Red Rock.'

'Why not? The folks there. …'

'I'm aimin' for Dodge City. That's where I was headed when I last stopped off at Red Rock. Don't reckon on stoppin' off there a second time.'

'Wa'al, leastways, we can ride together to the outskirts of town. Me, I'll be glad of yore company.' Beardsley paused and then, with the smile fading from his face, said quietly, 'Fore we set out, though, there's somethin' I gotta tell you.'

'Oh, an' what's that?'

'I ... I s'pose you ... you must've thought it kinda ironic that I should pump three bullets into the feller who once saved my life?'

'Nope.'

'Nope?'

'I don't figure Kane ever saved your life, Beardsley. Never did buy that story.'

'But. ...'

'He had some kinda hold over you, didn't he? That's why you bank-rolled him durin' his stay in Red Rock.'

'You've guessed it, Stone.' In the gathering gloom, Ben Beardsley's features were no longer clearly discernible, but Stone figured he was probably looking rather uncomfortable. Confession may be good for the soul, yet it is never easy. 'Kane and I were cell-mates at Claxton County Jail,' said the mayor. 'That was ten years ago. I was in for armed robbery. Served seven years. We shared that cell for 'bout three weeks, is all. Kane was startin' his sentence. I was finishin' mine.'

'Armed robbery, huh? That's pretty damn bad, Beardsley.'

'The name ain't Beardsley. It's Bradley. When I came outa jail, I decided to assume a new identity. An' it ain't as bad as it sounds. The armed robbery, I mean.'

'Nope?'

'No, it ain't. I was only twenty-two at the time. Got in with a pretty wild bunch. We didn't do nuthin' real bad. A li'l cattle-rustlin' was 'bout all. We never shot nobody. Nuthin' like that. Then, Davy Hope, he was older 'n the rest of us, got this idea of robbin' a bank. He said we oughta make some real money an', at the same time, earn a name for ourselves. Most of the others wanted to go along, but I wasn't so sure. Anyways, I was too scared to back out, so I stuck with 'em. I wish to hell I hadn't. The raid was a complete disaster. Davy Hope an' two others got theirselves killed an' one of the bank clerks was shot. Luckily he didn't die, or me an' the rest would've been hanged for sure. I swear to you, Stone, I didn't even draw my gun, but, even so, I have regretted that episode every day of my life since.'

'You paid for yore crime.'

'With seven years in jail? Huh, that was the easy part!'

'Don't worry, Beardsley, or should I call you Bradley?'

'Best leave it as Beardsley. I got used to that name now.'

'Wa'al, Beardsley, don't worry. I ain't gonna split on you.'

'I ain't worried 'bout that. Not any more. I bank-rolled Kane to keep his mouth shut, but that was a bad mistake.'

'Guess it was.'

'Sure it was. An' what's to stop someone else like Kane from ridin' into Red Rock an' recognisin' me?'

'It's a pretty big country, an' lightnin' don't usually strike the same spot twice.'

'Mebbe not, Stone, but I ain't takin' no chances. I'm gonna make a clean breast of my past to my wife an' children, to my parents-in-law an' to my fellow councillors on Red Rock town council.' Beardsley sighed heavily and went on, in a voice cracking with emotion, 'I could lose everythin' I hold dear. I know that. But I gotta be free of this terrible shadow that's hung over me all these years.'

Stone smiled sympathetically and laid a comforting hand on the other's shoulder.

'Reckon yo're makin' the right decision,' he said. 'An', if 'n' yore wife an' family don't stand up for you an' yore fellow-citizens don't re-elect you mayor at the next election, then I figure they ain't deservin' of you. Everyone's entitled to make a mistake an', in my book at least, yo're a good man, Ben Beardsley.'

The Kentuckian thrust out his huge mitt and the two men shook hands. Then, they walked in silence from the saloon.

A few minutes later, Beardsley was mounted on the late Travis Miller's gelding and Stone on his own. They trotted slowly away from the ghost town. Darkness had fallen and the stars glittered in the blue-black sky as the two men rode southwards.